THE MILLION DOLLAR KICK

DAN GUTMAN

Hyperion Paperbacks for Children

New York

Copyright © 2001 by Dan Gutman
All rights reserved. No part of this book may be reproduced or transmitted in any form or by any means, electronic or mechanical, including photocopying, recording, or by any information storage and retrieval system, without written permission from the publisher. For information address Hyperion Books for Children, 114 Fifth Ave, New York, New York 10011-5690.

First Hyperion Paperback edition, 2003

1 3 5 7 9 10 8 6 4 2
Printed in the United States of America

Library of Congress Cataloging-in-Publication Data
Gutman, Dan.
The million dollar kick / Dan Gutman.—1st ed.
　　p.　　cm.
Summary: Thirteen-year-old Whisper, who hates sports, is torn when she gets a chance to win a million dollars by kicking a goal against a local soccer hero.
ISBN 0-7868-0764-4 (trade)—ISBN 0-7868-2612-6 (lib.)
ISBN 0-7868-1584-1 (pbk.)
[1. Soccer—Fiction. 2. Contests—Fiction.] I. Title.
PZ7.G9846 Mg 2001
[Fic]—dc21
2001016958

Visit www.hyperionchildrensbooks.com

Also by Dan Gutman
The Million Dollar Shot
Virtually Perfect

To Debbie Licorish,
teacher of the year, in my book!

Thanks to my friends in Oklahoma,
as well as Geoff Chalkley, the Cossaboon family,
Jim Gavin, Rachel Trotta, Donna Bray,
and Shannon Dean.

Contents

My Mental Video

I have a memory that's stuck in my brain. It's like a song that you hear once on the radio and can't get out of your mind for the rest of the day. Sometimes I even dream it. It's my mental videotape.

It happened four years ago, when I was in third grade. I was playing my first soccer game. We were at the field over by Lake Overholser, not far from my house. Our team was called the Smiles, and we were sponsored by my orthodontist. There was a big smiling mouth on our jerseys.

Our team hadn't had much chance to practice or to get to know each other before the first game. I was the biggest girl on the team, so the coach figured I must be good and she put me in right away. I tried to tell her I had never played soccer before, but either she didn't hear me or she wasn't listening.

1

This is what my mental videotape looks like:

The game has just begun and the ball is near the middle of the field. A whole crowd of girls is around it, trying to kick it free. I'm hanging back away from the swarm a little. No way am I going to get myself into the middle of all those flailing arms and legs. Then, suddenly, the ball squirts out and bounces right to me.

For a few brief moments, the other girls don't seem to notice. They are still in a swarm, bumping and kicking each other.

"Take it, Whisper!" my mother screams from the sideline. "You're wide open, honey!"

I take a swipe at the ball with my foot, and by some miracle I don't miss. I dash after it downfield.

I have beaten all the defenders and there is nobody between me and the goal except for the goalie. I have a completely open shot. I wait until I am ten or fifteen feet from the goal. The ball rolls to a stop. Not taking any chances, I aim right at the middle of the goal. I plant my foot, and slam the ball as hard as I can.

Well, the ball doesn't go right at the middle. It must go off the side of my toe a little, because it sails to the right. I think I've messed up, but the goal is wider than I thought and the ball is heading right for the corner.

The goalie makes a desperate lunge at the ball, but she just can't reach it. It skips into the back of the net. I've scored! I can't believe it. I have never played soccer in my life, not even kicking the ball around the backyard, and I have scored on my first shot.

I pump my fist in the air and run back to accept the congratulations of my teammates for having kicked the first goal of our first game.

But nobody congratulates me. There is an eerie silence.

"Hey, stupid!" a girl on the other team hollers. "You kicked the ball into your own goal! Thanks a lot!"

I turn around. The girls on the other team are either laughing out loud or putting their hands over their faces to hide their laughter. The girls on my team just stare at me in disbelief. The coach is shaking her head. Nobody knows what to say. I look over at my mother on the sidelines. She has her hand over her eyes, like she wants to hide.

I don't even go back to the bench. I don't want to talk to any of my teammates. I don't want to hear them tell me everything is okay, or tell me that everybody makes mistakes, or tell me they still like me even though I have done THE STUPIDEST THING IN THE WORLD. I don't want to hear those lies.

I just run off the field and dash home, arriving around the same time as my mother. I rip off my uniform and my shin guards and throw them in the garbage. All I want to do is lie on my bed and cry.

I've watched my mental videotape hundreds of times. With my eyes closed, I can run it forward, backward, and in slow motion. I can even freeze-frame it. There's only one thing I can't do to my mental videotape. I can't erase it.

When I think back, sometimes I wonder if kicking that goal was the beginning of all my problems. That was the moment everything went wrong for me. That was the day I started to shut down. If I hadn't kicked that stupid goal, I bet the last four years would have turned out different. Maybe not. Who knows?

One thing for sure, though. I vowed at that moment that I would never play any sport ever again.

CHAPTER **2**

Whomperjawed

Late yesterday afternoon, I rode my bike by a grassy field a few blocks from my house that had been there as long as I could remember. But this time, bulldozers and earth-moving equipment were rumbling all over the place. I asked one of the workers what was going on, and he told me they were building a garden center.

"In other words," I said, "you're tearing up the grass to make a store that sells grass seed?"

"Sure 'nuff," he replied. He didn't seem to appreciate the irony of that. Nobody seems to notice what we're doing to the earth, or if they do notice, nobody seems to care.

The grassy field where they are building the garden center is at the edge of a wooded area. When I'm depressed or feeling lonely, or sometimes when

I just want to be alone to think, I ride my bike out to these woods. Sometimes I read. Sometimes I write in my journal. There's a big tree that I like to sit under. The sound of the wind rustling through the leaves is soothing.

Nobody ever comes out to the woods. At least I've never seen anybody out there. It seems like it's the only place left on earth where people haven't marched in and put up a fast-food restaurant or video store. The woods will be gone someday, I'll bet. They'll probably be turned into some ugly housing development or strip mall.

That's not really fair to say, I suppose. Oklahoma City probably doesn't have any more strip malls than any other American city. It's just that I live here, and it seems like every day there are fewer places where you can sit under a tree and more places where you can buy things.

I rode my bike out to the woods yesterday to think about what happened to me that morning. It was something that I didn't want to forget, ever. With all the excitement over, I finally had the chance to catch my breath and collect my thoughts. Years from now, if I ever have children of my own, they'll never believe what happened to me yesterday morning.

That soccer game back when I was eight was the first turning point in my life, I realized. What happened yesterday might have been the second. It's funny that soccer, a game I don't even particularly like, should play such an important role in my life.

I can't tell the story without first telling you a little bit about myself and my family. My dad is a pilot who flies jumbo jets out of Wiley Post Airport in Oklahoma City. I don't see him all that much because he's out of town a lot. Even when he's home, he's usually so jet-lagged that he sleeps away a good part of the day.

I remember when I was little, my dad and I could make fun of each other and laugh about it. I had a collection of Mr. Peanut figures, and he thought that was the silliest thing in the world. I would tease him, too. He used to bring home those little bags of pretzels they give out on his plane, and when we went on long car trips, I would make him pass them out like a flight attendant.

But once I got to be ten or eleven, I didn't like

being teased anymore. I stopped collecting the Mr. Peanut figures and we stopped joking with each other.

I have nothing against my dad, really. When I was little, we used to hold hands and wrestle and roughhouse and laugh a lot. But somewhere along the line as I got bigger, it seemed weird to be rolling around on a bed with my dad. Then it started feeling weird to hold hands with him in public, and after a while he didn't even hug me or put his arm around my shoulder anymore.

He didn't touch me the wrong way or anything like that. I want to make that clear. I guess we just grew apart from each other as I got older. Maybe it's just part of growing up. I feel bad about it, but I don't think there's anything either of us can do about it.

My mom, well, she's another story. A few years ago my mom was diagnosed with multiple sclerosis, this disease that slowly destroys your spinal cord. Nobody knows what causes it, and there's no cure for it. We never had a really close relationship, but after Mom got MS, things got worse.

When she was a girl, my mom was a great athlete. She could play any sport, and play it just as well as the boys in her neighborhood. That's what she tells me, and my uncle backs her up.

The thing is, when my mom was young, girls weren't allowed to play organized sports. Hard to believe today, but there was a time when there were no girls' basketball teams, no soccer for girls, or even softball. There were only teams for boys. This wasn't even illegal or anything! It was just the way things were. Back then, people didn't think girls wanted to play sports or were capable of competing.

This was the Stone Age, of course. The 1970s.

When my mom was in high school, the only "sport" that was open to her was cheerleading. She was a good cheerleader, but she has always said she wished she could have been out on the field, with somebody cheering for *her*.

By the time I was born, laws had been passed that made it illegal to discriminate against girls. Girls' sports were everywhere. Too late for my mom, of course. She was in a wheelchair.

Unfortunately, I didn't inherit any of my mother's athletic ability. I've always been the tallest girl in the class, but I can't run fast and my eyesight is poor.

I have this weird thing with my eyes. They don't work together. I'm never looking through both eyes at the same time. My left eye looks at close objects and my right eye looks at objects that are far away.

I never knew I had this problem until I went to the eye doctor for a checkup and he gave me this funny set of glasses with the picture of a chicken on one side and a picture of a cage on the other. People with normal vision see the chicken in the cage, but I saw a piece of chicken here, a part of the cage here. It was really confusing.

The eye doctor told me that my eyes work independently. This causes me to have poor "depth perception." Basically that means that when somebody throws a ball in my direction, it's likely to bounce off my head. Sports are not my thing.

But it's more than just eye-hand coordination. I could never seem to understand how games were played. When my mom signed me up for soccer in third grade (against my will, I'll have you know), I just didn't *get* it. The team played a couple of scrimmages, and I couldn't figure out what was going on. I didn't know who was on my side, or which direction we were supposed to be kicking the ball. All the other girls seemed to know right away exactly what to do, but everything I did was wrong.

"You're on defense!" the coach kept shouting to me. "Defense!"

Defense? I didn't even know what that meant. First, he'd told me I was on the blue team, and then he was telling me I was on the defense team. I was clueless.

It didn't take long to realize that I wasn't playing soccer for fun. I was playing because my mom wanted me to. I hated every second of it. After I kicked the ball into my own goal, I quit and didn't go back.

My theory is that Mom is disappointed in me because there are all these girls' sports teams I could play on, and I hate sports. She probably wishes she could be young *now*, so she could live her childhood all over again.

I guess maybe she takes it out on me. Just a guess, of course. I'm not a shrink or anything. But Mom and I are not close, and I think that's why.

My little sister, Briana, well, Mom just *adores* her. Briana is in fourth grade and she loves anything to do with sports. She plays soccer and basketball, and she's the only girl on her Little League base-ball team. Sports posters are plastered all over the walls of her room. Trophies and souvenirs line the bookshelves. She knows lots of meaningless statis-tics. Briana will even watch *bowling* on TV. If *that's* not a waste of time, I don't know what is.

If you ask me, sports are just stupid anyway. At the beginning of the year, in English, my teacher Mrs. Knowles assigned the class to write a three-hundred-word essay in which we had to argue against something. We could choose anything in the world. Other kids wrote their essays about smoking, curfews, school uniforms, racism, and things like that. I wrote about sports. I kept a copy of my essay. . . .

SPORTS ARE A WASTE
By Whisper Nelson

Why is it that this whole country is totally obsessed with hitting, kicking, and throwing balls at nets, goals, and hoops? It seems that if we're not playing some silly game, we are watching one on television. Don't we have anything

better to do with our time? What
does this say about us as a
civilization?

Soccer, baseball, football,
basketball, and hockey are bad
enough. But several of the boys
in my class are hopelessly
devoted to NASCAR, which I
understand is some form of
automobile racing. Tell me, what
could be more pointless than
watching cars drive around and
around in circles? Why don't we
call this "sport" what it really
is—a waste of gasoline?

Sometime within the next
hundred years, the earth is
going to run out of oil. There
just won't be any more left.
What are we going to tell our
grandchildren when they ask why
we used gas to race cars around
and around in circles?

The earth has very serious
environmental problems. Global
warming. Overpopulation.
Extinction. Water shortages. The
temperature of the earth warmed up
something like ten degrees in the

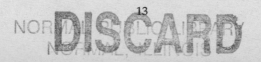

twentieth century. It will be even worse this century.

Think of all the natural resources we waste building sports stadiums. Think of all the chemicals we dump on the ground so people can play silly games on soft, green grass.

Believe me, one of these days you're going to turn on the faucet in your bathroom or kitchen and nothing will come out. One of these days you're going to flick on your TV and the screen will stay dark. One of these days you're going to pull up to a gas station and be told there is no gas to pump . . . at any price. You'll be sitting there with your tennis racquets, golf clubs, and basketball in the backseat. And it will be too late to do anything about it. All you cared about was sports, when you should have been paying attention to the planet.

Welcome to the future. A future with no water, no clean air, no gas, no electricity, and

no sports. We'll all be dead. I
hope the sports fans will be happy.

I never thought Mrs. Knowles was going to have some of us read our essays in front of the class, but she did. And one of the ones she chose was mine.

Well, almost as soon as the title was out of my mouth, boys in the class actually started booing and throwing things (especially the NASCAR idiots, who are as dumb as a box of rocks and sit in the back of the room).

But I didn't care. Mrs. Knowles gave me the highest mark in the class because she said I showed "passion" about my subject.

"Whisper is passionate!" somebody cracked, causing the NASCAR idiots to be convulsed with giggling. Middle-school boys can be so immature.

"Yeah, I reckon she's in love with a tree," Dan Mills snickered.

He would never admit it to anyone, but Dan Mills asked me out last year. He had been trying to get my attention for a long time by poking holes in various parts of his body. He's so pathetic, it's sad. First he pierced an ear and asked me if I liked it. I told him I couldn't care less, so the next day he pierced the other ear. I pretended not to notice. The following week he had poked some disgusting thing through his nose and stuck it right in my face and asked me to go to the mall with him.

"You can jam a shovel through your head," I told him. "I don't go to malls."

Ever since I said that, Dan has been giving me a hard time. When he said I was in love with a tree, I slid down into my seat and tried to think of ways to sneak out of the class without anyone noticing. But then I was saved.

"She's right, you know," somebody said.

I looked up. It was Jess Kirby, a boy who sits two rows over and one seat in front of mine. The only reason I had been able to survive the humiliation of middle school was because Jess Kirby was even more geeky than I am.

He was the stereotypical science nerd, right down to the glasses. He didn't wear a plastic pocket protector or anything, but he did carry a laptop computer wherever he went. He used it to record the results of his "scientific experiments." One time some of the other boys hid his laptop under the bleachers in the gym and the whole seventh grade got detention.

"The fact is," Jess told the class, "the four warmest years of the twentieth century all occurred in the nineteen-nineties. The earth is warming up at an alarming rate, and if we don't do something about it, it will become uninhabitable."

"Oooh, Kirby is in love with Whisper Nelson," one of the NASCAR idiots cracked, and everybody laughed. I know I should keep my mouth shut, but sometimes I just can't help it.

"Why don't you jerks grow up?" I barked.

"Oooh, Whisper is standing up for Kirby! She's in *loooooove!*"

The bell rang at that point and everybody rushed to lunch, like a bunch of sheep being herded into a pen. I probably should have thanked Jess for bailing me out, but I had enough problems without having everybody think I liked Jess Kirby.

Here's the way it is in my school: you're "in" or you're "out." If you're thin, you're in. If you're cute and blond, you're in. It helps if your parents have money and buy nice stuff with it. The in girls all have lots of friends, and they flit around together like birds, whispering, spreading rumors, and telling lies about the girls who aren't in. All they care about is who said what, who wore what, and who liked whom.

Needless to say, I'm "out." I had some friends when I was in elementary school, but as soon as we got into middle school they mysteriously became all giggly and stupid, caring only about looks and makeup and clothes and boys. My only friend in middle school was Linda Gann, but she moved away and we lost touch.

My mother said I should join a club to meet people, so I joined the chess club. But it was all boys except for me. I didn't want to lose to them, but when I beat them, they got obnoxious. So I quit.

The other way to get "in," it seems, is to be good at sports. I don't like to admit it, but part of the reason why I hate sports so much is probably that I'm lousy at them. I've always been tall and "big-boned," which I think is just another way of saying "fat" without saying "fat." In gym class they always made us run, and I always came in last.

Around fourth grade, kids started teasing me. I remember one day we were doing the fifty-yard dash and this boy asked me if I played piano. I said no, and asked him why. He said, "Because when you run, it looks like you're carrying one."

Everybody thought that was the funniest thing they'd ever heard. I ran home crying.

I think I've mentioned just about everything that is wrong with me. Oh, one more thing. I'm hideous-looking. My hair is all stringy and a lot of times I think there's no point in combing it because it looks just as awful combed. I dyed it red once, but it looked stupid and everybody made fun of me.

Did you ever hear the word *whomperjawed*? When something is whomperjawed, it doesn't fit quite right. Like a jar with a lid that's just a little bit too big. I feel like I'm a whomperjawed human being.

A few days after school started, I was in the bathroom and one of the in girls came in. When I came out of the stall, she was putting on makeup. Personally, I don't wear makeup, and I won't wear dresses or fancy clothes (no matter how many times my mom begs me to). It just seems superficial to care so much about your personal appearance. Anyway, I guess I made a face as I passed her, and she saw me in the mirror.

"What's got you so *aggravated*, Nelson?"

"They test cosmetics on bunnies, you know," I informed her. "They kill innocent animals so girls can make themselves look pretty."

The girl turned around and looked at me up and down.

"You know what your problem is, Whisper Nelson?"

"What?" I asked defiantly.

"You hate yourself," she said. "It's obvious."

And I couldn't argue with her.

CHAPTER 3

Rules and Rip-offs

My sister Briana got straight As on her last report card (as usual), so Mom said she could have the special treat of her choice. Of course, getting straight As in fourth grade isn't exactly like winning the Nobel Prize. Wait until Briana gets to seventh grade, when she'll have to learn algebra and geometry and all that other incomprehensible stuff.

For her treat, Briana chose to go to Donut City, which is a big chain out here in Oklahoma. I was assigned to take her because it's hard for Mom to get around and Briana's not old enough to go by herself.

"Donut City?" I asked, astonished. "I thought your idea of a treat was a chocolate protein bar."

To keep her energy level up for sports, Briana

21

pretty much lives on health food. I thought she would sooner swallow poison than junk food.

"Once I year, I like to go insane," she explained.

Behind the counter at Donut City, they have just about every kind of doughnut in existence. I ordered a powdered-sugar doughnut for myself and Briana got a Bavarian cream, the gooeyest doughnut they had. She gobbled it down like someone who had been stranded for weeks on a desert island with no food, so I bought her another one.

"Look, there's Carmen Applegate," she said as she licked the cream off her fingertips.

I figured one of Briana's little ponytailed friends had come in, but she was pointing to a life-size cardboard cutout of a soccer player that was propped up near the counter. The soccer player was holding a sign that said KICK ONE PAST ME AND WIN A MILLION BUCKS.

"Who's Carmen Applegate?" I asked.

Briana looked at me like I was the dumbest person in the world.

"Are you joking?" she asked. "You really don't know who Carmen Applegate is? She's like the most famous keeper in the world."

"A zookeeper?"

"Goalkeeper!" Briana exclaimed. "She's the star of the Oklahoma City Kick."

"Never heard of 'em." We had finished our doughnuts and I was ready to go home.

"Do you live in a cave?" Briana said. "The Kick are a professional women's soccer team."

I didn't even know there *was* professional women's soccer, and I couldn't care less about it. But Briana dashed over to the cardboard cutout to pick up one of the brochures. This is what it said. . . .

THE MILLION DOLLAR KICK

So you say you're a pretty good shot, eh? Well, do you think you can kick one past *me*? The Oklahoma City Kick, in association with *The Daily Oklahoman* and Donut City, will be selecting one lucky soccer fan to try.

On June fifth, before our game against the Colorado Rapids, that fan will get the chance to kick a twenty-yard penalty shot. No defenders. If that shooter can get it past me, he or she will win one million dollars. If I stop the ball, the prize is a year's supply of delicious Donut City doughnuts. So either way, you win.

What do you say? Wanna try? The only thing standing between you and a million dollars is . . . me.

"I'm gonna win!" Briana announced, already reaching for a pen to fill out the entry form.

Briana is ridiculously optimistic . . . about everything. She always assumes she's going to win. She never gets depressed or down on herself. Most of the time, she's happy as a gopher in soft dirt.

I suspect she's just too young to understand how much disappointment and failure life throws at you. There's a world of difference between the ages of ten and thirteen. I know from experience. When I was little, I was perky and enthusiastic about everything all the time, too.

"Forget about it," I suggested. "You're wasting your time. Let's get out of here."

I set Briana straight. I told her that companies just hold these stupid contests so people will fill out a card and give them their name and address. Then they can put together a big mailing list so they can send you junk mail and call you up on the phone and try to sell you stuff you don't want.

"I don't care," she said. "I'm gonna win."

I told her the contest was obviously a desperate attempt to generate interest in the Oklahoma City Kick. Probably their attendance is down and if they don't attract more fans, they'll go out of business or have to move to another city.

"I don't care," Briana insisted.

I told her that she had a one-in-a-zillion chance to get picked to take the shot. And if this Carmen Applegate was that good a goalie, the winner would have a one-in-a-million chance to score on her.

"Somebody's gonna win the contest," Briana rebutted. "It might as well be me. And I can nail a twenty-yard kick with my eyes closed. I don't care who the keeper is."

"There's gotta be a catch," I sighed. "There always is."

Briana filled out the entry form and turned it over. On the flip side of the form, it said in big letters: Dream Up a New Slogan for the Kick!

Apparently, part of the contest was to invent a slogan that the Kick could use in their advertising and promotions. The kid who came up with the best slogan would win the contest and get to take the Million Dollar Kick.

"That's a rip-off!" Briana protested.

I explained to her that it wasn't a rip-off. Technically, the word *rip-off* means that you were overcharged for something. Briana didn't even have to *buy* anything. But I knew what she meant. Briana had thought the contest was simply a random drawing.

Unlike me, my sister loves a challenge. She furrowed her brow and set herself to the task of coming up with a slogan that would win the contest. The current slogan for the Kick was "We Get a Kick Out of You," which Briana and I both agreed was hopelessly lame.

"How about 'The Kick Are OK?'" Briana suggested, already poised to write it down on the form. "Get it? OK? Oklahoma?"

"OK is not exactly high praise,'" I explained. "You think they're going to pick a slogan that says the team is mediocre?"

Briana was not discouraged. "How about 'Our Goal Is to Win?'" she suggested.

"Color me excited," I replied tactfully.

Briana closed her eyes and leaned her head back, as if the perfect slogan was going to drop down from the heavens into her brain.

I wasn't going to waste my time dreaming up

a slogan for the Kick. I mean, I couldn't care less about the Kick or their stupid slogan. But did you ever try *not* to think of something? Like, if somebody told you to *not* think of a pink elephant floating over the Statue of Liberty, the first image that would pop into your mind would be a pink elephant floating over the Statue of Liberty, right?

So, on some subconscious level, no matter how hard I tried not to, my brain started working on a slogan for the Kick. I tried to remember soccer terms that could be made into a pun.

Score . . . goal . . . net . . . foot . . . kick . . .

Almost immediately, the perfect slogan came to me.

"I got it," I announced.

"What is it?" Briana asked.

"The Kick . . . Kick Butt."

Briana grinned at me in that innocent, fourth-grade, easily impressed way.

"You're a genius!" she exclaimed, and excitedly wrote "The Kick Kick Butt" on the entry form.

"I hope you win," I said, looking over the form to make sure she filled in the name, address, and phone number correctly.

"Oh, I'm gonna win," she said confidently.

It appeared that Briana had filled in all the blanks on the entry form. I was going to give it back to her when I noticed the tiny disclaimer at the bottom of the page. A disclaimer is those legal words they print in tiny type that says you can't sue them no matter what sleazy thing they do to you:

You Must Be Between the Ages of 12 and 16 to Enter.

"What?" Briana complained. "That's a rip-off!"

"It can't be a rip-off," I explained calmly. "If you didn't pay for something, you can't be ripped off."

"You know what I mean!"

"Rules are rules," I pointed out. "It's their contest and they can run it any way they want. Don't have a conniption over it."

Miss Happy was about as worked up as I've ever seen her. She said it wasn't fair, except she used some words that you only hear in R-rated movies and on the playground when there are no grown-ups around.

"Why don't we put *your* name on the form?" Briana said after she had calmed down again.

"Then if you win, I'll take the kick."

I could have told my sister we could never get away with that. The people who run these contests are professionals. They've got lawyers and legal departments. They would never let one person win the contest and another person take the shot. If that were legal, the winner could simply hire a professional soccer player to take the shot.

But I figured the chances of winning were so slim, it really didn't matter whose name was on the form. We weren't going to win anyway. I was sick of hanging around Donut City and just wanted to go home. I told Briana to go ahead and put whatever she wanted on the form.

She carefully scratched out "Briana Nelson" and wrote "Whisper Nelson" in its place. Then she went over to the cardboard cutout of Carmen Applegate, crossed her fingers for good luck, and dropped the entry form into the slot.

CHAPTER 4

A Million Dollars Is a Million Dollars

"Howdy."

"May I speak with Miss Whisper Nelson, please?"

That was the first of several surprises that happened one day a few weeks later. Usually, when the phone rings, it's one of Briana's little friends inviting her over to play. It's very rare that the phone rings and it's for me.

It was a man's voice on the phone. I didn't recognize him. Mom always tells us to be very careful when strangers call or show up at the door.

"Whisper is busy right now," I replied. "Who is this?"

"My name is Joe Fine," the guy said. "I work in the promotions department of *The Daily Oklahoman*."

I hung up.

If there's one thing I can't stand, it's telemarketers. Why do these jerks think they have the right to call you any time of the night or day to sell you things? I used to be polite to them, but when you tell them "no" politely, they just keep trying to convince you that you should buy whatever it is that they're selling. They never give up no matter what you say. So I started hanging up on them. Besides, my mom and dad already subscribe to *The Oklahoman*.

A few seconds after I hung up, the phone rang again. I figured it was probably the same guy, and I thought about just letting the answering machine pick it up. But there was the outside chance that Mom or Dad was calling, and it might be important. I wished we had Caller ID, but my parents didn't want to pay for it.

"Hello?"

"Miss, this is Joe Fine. I need to speak with Whisper Nelson—"

"We already *get* your paper," I snapped. "Take us off your mailing list, and please stop calling this number." I hung up the phone again.

That's usually the end of it. Once you tell these telemarketers in no uncertain terms that you're not interested, they usually leave you alone. At least for a couple of days, anyway. But a few seconds later, the phone rang for a *third* time. This Joe Fine guy was really getting on my nerves.

"Look, Mr. Fine," I said, after picking up the phone, "I told you nicely that we're not interested. What do I have to do to get you people to stop? Do I have to call the police?"

"I'm not selling anything!" he said quickly. "I need to speak with Whisper Nelson. It's very important."

"What's it about?" I asked.

"Are you Whisper Nelson?"

"Yeah," I admitted.

"Are you the Whisper Nelson who entered the Million Dollar Kick Contest at the Donut City on North Rockwell Avenue?"

I had to think for a moment. It had been weeks since Briana and I had been to Donut City. I had forgotten all about it. Searching my memory, I recalled that Briana had filled out a form to enter some silly contest and put my name on it because she wasn't old enough to enter.

"That was me, yes," I told Mr. Fine.

"Well, Miss Nelson, I have good news for you. You're the winner!"

I sat down at the kitchen table. I never won any-thing before in my life. When I was younger I used to enter contests all the time. Then I learned in sta-tistics at school that the odds were so ridiculous that you had about as much chance of winning as you had of growing a third hand. So I stopped wasting my time entering contests.

"Hello?" Joe Fine asked.

This couldn't be happening, I told myself. I took a napkin off the table and wiped my forehead with it.

"Miss Nelson, are you still there?" he asked.

"Uh . . . yeah."

"Well, I'm happy to tell you that more than sixty thousand entries were received in the Million Dollar Kick Contest. One thousand of them were selected at random, and your slogan 'The Kick Kick Butt' was chosen as the best of them all! In fact, we already hired an advertising agency to create songs, T-shirts, billboards, and commercials using your slogan. So on June fifth, you'll have the chance to take a single shot against the Kick goal-keeper Carmen Applegate for a million dollars! Isn't that exciting?"

I looked at the calendar on the refrigerator. It was April fifth. Two months. I wiped my forehead again with the napkin. It would take a while to process the information.

"Hello? Miss Nelson? I suppose you're in shock. That's perfectly normal under the circumstances. It's not every day—"

"I'll ponder it," I finally said.

"You'll ponder what?"

"I'll ponder whether or not I want to take the kick."

Mr. Fine didn't say anything for a second or two. I guess he wasn't expecting to hear that.

"Is this *really* Whisper Nelson?" he asked.

"I *told* you it is."

"And you entered the Million Dollar Kick Contest, right?"

"You could say that."

"But . . . you aren't sure if you *want* to take the shot?"

"I said I'd ponder it," I repeated. "I don't like to make snap decisions. Is that okay?"

"I . . . suppose so," he said.

"Good. Can you call back tomorrow?"

"Sure. I'll call you around four o'clock tomorrow afternoon."

I hung up the phone and wiped my forehead

again. The napkin was soaked with sweat.

I was glad that nobody was home except me. I could sit and think about what had happened without having to explain it to anyone.

A rush of emotions was going through me. Not that money was all that important to me, but a million dollars *was* a million dollars. Even if I didn't spend money on clothes or jewelry or stuff like that, a million dollars would send me to college someday. And Briana, too. Anybody would want to win a million dollars. And all I would have to do would be to kick a stupid soccer ball twenty yards into a net.

That was the part I felt uneasy about. I couldn't kick a soccer ball for beans. I was the worst soccer player in the world when I was in third grade, and I hadn't touched a soccer ball since then. The chances of my being able to kick one past a professional goalie were probably between zero and none.

Not only that, but I would have to make the kick in front of a lot of people. I'm not exactly the kind of person who likes to be the center of attention. I don't even like it when people *look* at me. If I agreed to take the kick, thousands of spectators would be watching.

Plus, everybody at school would certainly find out about it. The NASCAR idiots would be in their glory, having something *else* they could ridicule me about.

No, it would be insane to take the kick. When the guy called again, I'd tell him I wasn't interested, I decided. He could pick somebody else to take the kick. Somebody who wanted to do it more than I did.

But . . . a million dollars *was* a million dollars. How many people—in their entire lifetimes—ever get the chance to win a million dollars?

I grabbed another napkin and wiped my forehead with it.

"So," Dad said as we sat down to dinner that night, "what did you all do today?"

When Dad is out of town, Mom usually lets me and Briana watch TV while we eat dinner. But Dad thinks it's important that we all sit around the dinner table "as a family" and "review the day." My guess is that he feels guilty about being away from home so much, and he tries to make up for it when he's there. But that's just a theory. I'm not a shrink or anything.

"I hit a ball that bounced off the fence during batting practice," Briana announced cheerfully.

"Way to go, slugger!" Dad said, clapping Briana on the back.

"I picked out the wallpaper for the upstairs bathroom," reported Mom.

My mother spends most of her time making "improvements" on our house. She improves everything she can improve upon, and after she can't make any more improvements, she talks my dad into selling the house and moving. Then she gets to work making improvements on the *new* house. People think she's a good decorator. I say she's got a psychological inability to be satisfied with anything. Just a theory, of course. As I said, I'm no shrink.

"What about you, Whisper?" Dad asked. "What did you do today?"

Usually I say, "Nothing." Then Dad starts giving me a hard time, insisting that I come up with at least one interesting thing I did during the day. I'll say, "I discovered the cure for cancer" or something ridiculous and we'll move on to another topic of conversation.

"I won a contest," I informed everybody.

"Oh, some contest at school, honey?" Dad asked.

"No. A contest at Donut City."

Briana looked up from her plate.

"Remember when Briana and I were there a few weeks ago? Well, they had this contest where you have to make up a slogan and somebody will get the chance to kick a soccer ball into a goal and win a million dollars. A guy called up on the phone this afternoon and told me my slogan won."

Mom and Dad stared at me, like they weren't sure if I was joking or not.

"Very funny, Whisper," Briana snorted.

"I mean it."

"You're lying."

"I'm not lying."

"Swear it's true."

"I swear it's true."

"Swear it on your grave."

"I swear it on my grave."

"Swear it on Grandma's—"

"Enough swearing!" Mom said. "Are you serious, Whisper? Did you really win this contest?"

"Sure 'nuff," I insisted.

"That's wonderful! What was your slogan?"

"The Kick Kick Butt."

"Oh dear." Mom groaned. "Was it really necessary to use the word *butt*? It's not a very nice word."

"She could have said, 'The Kick Kick A—,'" Briana noted.

"Briana!" warned Dad.

"Well, they picked it out of a thousand entries," I said. "And on June fifth, I can take the shot."

"That's a rip-off!" Briana whined. "*I* was the one who wanted to enter the contest. I could make the shot, easy. You don't even *play* soccer."

Little Miss Happy was aggravated. She even put on her "mad" face. She scrunches up her eyes, nose, and mouth and thinks we'll all feel sorry for her.

"What are you so upset about?" I asked her. "*You* put my name on the entry form. I would have chucked it in the trash."

"I should get the million dollars," Briana said. "What are you going to spend it on? Ripped blue jeans and T-shirts?"

Briana really cares about the way she looks and spends hours picking her clothes out. Me, I couldn't care less. I could have given her a piece of my mind. But I didn't. She *is* my sister and I *do* love her.

Sometimes I have to remind myself that ten-year-olds let dumb things escape from their mouths before they think them over.

"Anyway," I said casually, "I didn't say I was going to take the shot. I just said I won the contest."

"What?!" Briana demanded. Now she was really upset. "You mean you're not going to take the kick? You won the contest and you're not going to shoot?"

"Probably not," I said.

"It's a million bucks!"

"So what? It's just money."

"You're nuts!"

"It's entirely up to you, honey," Dad told me. "I think you're old enough to make up your own mind."

I looked over at Mom. The whole time I was arguing with Briana, Mom kept exchanging these worried glances with Dad, which said to me they would be talking it over in private later that night. My mom actually looked relieved when I said I had pretty much decided not to try the kick.

Briana insisted that I was totally out of my mind. Anybody who had the chance to win a million dollars with one kick and turned it down had to be insane, she claimed.

"What did you tell the man on the phone?" Mom asked.

"I told him I'd ponder it and give him an answer tomorrow."

Between my parents' bedroom and my bedroom is a vent in the wall where the heat comes out in the winter and the air-conditioning comes out in the summer. My parents don't know it, but through that vent I can hear most of what they say in their bedroom.

Later that night, I just happened to be on my hands and knees next to the vent. Well, okay, I was eavesdropping on my parents' conversation. This is what I was able to make out. . . .

DAD: She's thirteen years old. She can make up her own mind about this.

MOM: I'm afraid she'll be setting herself up for a colossal failure. What if she makes a fool of herself? She's so fragile emotionally.

DAD: Oh, I don't know. It might be fun for her, an experience she'll always

remember. Think of it as a life lesson.
And who knows, maybe she'll score
the goal. A million bucks would be
nice.

MOM: She's no good at sports.

DAD: If she tried, she might be good.

MOM: She won't try. Briana tries.
Whisper figures if she doesn't try,
she can't fail.

DAD: But how is she going to find out
what she's good at if she doesn't try?

MOM: Your guess is as good as mine.

So, they think I'm no good. They think I don't
try. I *hate* it when my parents make decisions about
me. Nobody can decide I'm not good at anything.
Nobody can tell me I don't try.

That's when I decided I was going to go through
with the Million Dollar Kick.

CHAPTER 5

Me Against Everybody Else

Less than an hour after I told the guy from *The Daily Oklahoman* that I had decided to go ahead and take the Million Dollar Kick, the doorbell rang. I peeked through the curtains and saw some lady standing on the front steps. She was well dressed, about my mom's age.

"I'll get it!" Briana shouted from upstairs. "It must be Jennifer picking me up for the game."

Briana bounded down the steps three at a time. She was wearing her soccer uniform and had a soccer ball in her arms. She threw open the door and was surprised to see it wasn't her friend Jennifer.

"I'll bet you're Whisper Nelson!" the lady said to Briana enthusiastically.

"No, *that's* Whisper over there," Briana said, pointing at me.

43

The moment the lady turned to me, the smile vanished from her face as if somebody had flipped a switch to turn it off.

"Oh," she said, "My name is Bobbie Frisk. I'm a reporter for *The Daily Oklahoman*. I was told you are the winner of the Million Dollar Kick Contest and I'd like to ask you a few questions."

"No thanks," I said. The last thing I wanted was for kids at school to see a newspaper article about me.

"You can interview *me*," Briana suggested, all smiles and cuteness.

My mom shouted from the kitchen. "Is Jennifer here to pick Briana up?"

"No, it's a lady from the newspaper," Briana hollered back.

Mom rolled out of the kitchen, drying her hands on a towel. She shook hands with the newspaper lady, who told her she was assigned to interview me. Mom was embarrassed, because I hadn't even told her about my decision to go through with the Million Dollar Kick.

"Please come in," Mom told the reporter. "I made some coffee. Would you like a cup?"

"Thank you, yes."

Oh, man! A cup of coffee meant the lady would be in our house for fifteen minutes at least. I wished my mom would have the good sense to say we didn't want any publicity. That's what I would have done.

A car horn honked outside, and Briana went running off to her game. Mom went to pour the coffee, leaving me and the reporter alone.

"Aren't you supposed to call before knocking on somebody's door?" I asked. "Don't you need a search warrant or something?"

I wanted her to know from the start that I would be a tough interview. But she just laughed.

"Search warrants are for the police. I just want to chat with you a little, Whisper. I came over here because it's too easy for people to say no over the telephone. I prefer to take my chances on a face-to-face visit."

Well, she was right there. If she had called on the phone, I might have hung up on her, and that would have been the end of it.

"So," she said, pulling out a pad and pen, "Whisper is certainly an unusual name. Why don't you start by telling me where it came from?"

"I don't know," I replied coldly.

"Really? You never asked your parents?"

"No."

I knew exactly why my parents named me Whisper. I just didn't feel like telling her. Mom rolled back in with two cups of coffee and a glass of apple juice for me. She's always trying to get me to drink apple juice because it supposedly contains a lot of vitamins. I resolved not to touch it no matter how thirsty I became.

"When I was in the hospital holding Whisper the day after she was born," Mom recalled, "we still hadn't given her a name yet. But she kept moving her mouth and making these soft noises that sounded a little like somebody whispering. So my husband suggested we name her 'Whisper.'"

"That's adorable!" the reporter chimed, writing it all down.

I rolled my eyes. I hate the name Whisper. I always have. I would rather my parents had named me "Cow Dung" than "Whisper."

"So tell me, Whisper. How do you feel about getting the chance to take the Million Dollar Kick?"

"Do I really have to answer these questions?" I asked. "Don't I have the right to remain silent like on TV?"

"You're not under arrest," Bobbie Frisk joked.

"Whisper, you be nice," my mother said sternly. "If you agreed to take the kick, then you have to do everything that goes with it."

No matter what I said to Bobbie Frisk, she kept smiling at me. Despite the smile, I didn't think she liked me. Smiling all the time must be part of the job description for a newspaper reporter. I made a mental note not to grow up and become one.

"Thank you, Mrs. Nelson," Bobbie Frisk told Mom. "Would you mind if Whisper and I talked privately for a few minutes?"

"Not at all," Mom said, and she shot me a look before rolling back to the kitchen.

"I guess you're a pretty good soccer player, huh?" Bobbie Frisk asked.

"No. I don't play."

"Did you *ever* play?"

"I played one game," I admitted. "When I was little."

"But you must *like* the game."

"Not particularly. My sister put my name on the entry form because she wasn't old enough to enter the contest."

"Really?" She seemed interested in that, and wrote something on her pad. I tried to read it, but couldn't make out her handwriting. "What don't you like about soccer?"

"I just think it's a moronic game. You run up and down a field kicking a ball for no apparent reason. I mean, what's the point? You can't even use your hands."

"That's fascinating!"

It didn't seem so fascinating to me. But she wrote everything down frantically, as if I were saying something important. She said somebody who didn't even *like* soccer winning the chance to take a million dollar kick was a great "angle," whatever that meant.

I had to answer a bunch of other dumb questions, like what grade I was in and what was the name of my school. Then she asked if I had anything to add before she wrapped up the interview.

"Yeah," I said. "Instead of writing silly soccer stories, why don't you write about something important?"

"Like what, Whisper?"

"Like the vanishing rain forest. Like the hole in the ozone layer. Did you know that the earth warmed up like ten degrees in the last hundred years? *That's* what you should be writing about. *That's* what's important. I mean, soccer is just a silly game. Nobody will be able to play it after our planet becomes uninhabitable."

She kept writing in her pad.

"Thank you, Whisper," she said, sticking out her hand. "I'll think about that suggestion. Good luck with the Million Dollar Kick."

"Whatever."

Two days later, the article appeared on the front page of *The Daily Oklahoman*. They even included my plug-ugly class photo, which they somehow managed to get their hands on. This is the article. . . .

RELUCTANT 7TH GRADER TO TAKE "THE MILLION DOLLAR KICK"

By BOBBIE FRISK
Special to The Daily Oklahoman

OKLAHOMA CITY, April 8: Her name may be Whisper, but on June 5, thousands of soccer fans will be screaming it at the top of their lungs.

That's when 13-year-old Whisper Nelson of

Oklahoma City will have a shot—one shot—at a million dollars. Miss Nelson, a seventh grader at Wilson Middle School, was selected from among many thousands of soccer fans as the winner of the contest sponsored by Donut City. If she can kick a ball past Oklahoma Kick star goalkeeper Carmen Applegate, Whisper Nelson will pocket a cool one million dollars. If she misses, well, she'll never have to buy another doughnut.

The amazing thing is, Whisper Nelson has only played soccer once in her life. That was several years ago. She doesn't play on a team, and she doesn't watch soccer on TV. And believe it or not, she doesn't even like the sport.

"I just think it's a moronic game," she says. "You run up and down a field kicking a ball for no apparent reason. I mean, what's the point? You can't even use your hands."

Miss Nelson, a quiet and serious young lady, has little time for games. She has far more important things than soccer on her mind. Things like the vanishing rain forest and the hole in the ozone layer. Not many young people can rattle off environmental statistics. Did you know that the earth warmed up by ten degrees in the 20th century? Whisper does.

"That's what's important," Whisper told The Daily Oklahoman. "Soccer is just a silly game. Nobody will be able to play it after our planet becomes uninhabitable."

Hopefully, the planet will still be inhabitable on June 5, when Whisper Nelson gets the chance of a lifetime to put one in the net at Taft Stadium. We'll be watching.

When I picked the morning paper off the front lawn and read that, I thought I was going to *die*. The reporter never told me she was going to print that stuff about the environment! I was just telling her what she *should* be writing about instead of silly sport stories. I was giving her career advice.

What a fool I was to speak with the press at all. They always get everything wrong. When that reporter knocked on our door, I should have just run upstairs, locked my door, and hid in my room. That's what I did after I saw the article in the paper.

"Whisper," my mother called through the door. "You're going to be late for school."

"I'm not going."

"Why? Aren't you feeling well?"

"Look at the newspaper."

Mom went to read the article and came back to my room.

"This is *wonderful*, Whisper!" she called through the door. "You're a celebrity! I have to get some copies to send to your aunts and uncles."

"Do you have any idea," I pointed out, "what the kids at school are going to say when they see that article? They're going to ruin my life. They're going to crucify me."

"Don't be silly," Mom scoffed. "They're going to be very impressed. They'll probably be asking you for your autograph."

Well, Mom was right. The first thing that happened when I walked into school was that somebody asked me for an autograph. It was Dan Mills. He turned around, pulled down his pants, and asked me to autograph his behind. Right in the hallway! His friends, the NASCAR idiots, fell all over themselves laughing.

I really should have stayed home from school that day. All day long, I felt like everybody was looking at me like I was a circus freak or something. When I walked through the hall between classes, I could hear kids whispering. Probably about me.

Nobody clapped me on the back and congratulated me for winning the contest. They just gave me a harder time than they usually do.

In science, Mr. McGrath held up the newspaper and showed the class the article. I sank into my seat, trying to disappear. Mr. McGrath said this would be a good opportunity to have a class discussion about the environment.

"I read on the Internet that global warming is a

big hoax," one of the girls said.

"So what if the earth is a couple of degrees warmer, anyway?" some guy said. "It's no big deal."

"Yeah," one of the NASCAR idiots agreed. "That means we'll get a longer summer vacation."

Everybody laughed except me. The two boys high-fived each other.

"Whisper," Mr. McGrath said. "What do *you* think?"

"I think summer vacation won't be much fun when there's no clean air to breathe and no clean water to drink."

"I'll drink beer," one of the NASCAR idiots cracked, and again everybody but me laughed.

"Beer is made from water, moron," I felt compelled to inform him.

"Hey," a blond girl named Anna Evans said. "What have *you* ever done for the environment, besides complain about it?"

"Yeah, I don't see you hugging any trees or holding any rallies," another girl added.

"Yeah," most of the class echoed.

Just like always, it was me against everybody else. It was *always* me against everybody else. Even when I was *right*, it was me against everybody else.

I looked around and noticed that Jess Kirby, that science dweeb, was absent. If he had been there, he would probably have made some comment supporting me, and they would have been making fun of *him*.

In the middle of math class, when Mrs. Connolly was facing the blackboard, a folded-up piece of paper hit me on the shoulder and landed on my desk. I opened it up. This is what it said:

Hey, Nelson, you want to do something good for the environment? Why don't you put a bag over your head? You're like ugly on an ape.

I didn't know who wrote the note. It didn't matter. I ripped the paper up into little pieces, cursing the day I let Briana talk me into putting my name on that stupid contest entry form. I had enough aggravation, enough humiliation in my life without having to deal with this.

What had happened? When we were little kids in first and second grade, a lot of these jerks who were tormenting me were my friends. We used to play together. I was even friends with some of the boys. Even a few of the NASCAR idiots. They were nice back then. What happened?

I was thinking about all this in the lunchroom when that science dweeb, Jess Kirby, came over to me. I was sitting at a table by myself. In my school, there's a geek table, a jock table, a prep table, and a punk table. I usually grab a table of my own so I don't have to talk to any of them.

"I thought you were absent," I said.

"I had a dentist appointment," Jess replied, standing there awkwardly with his laptop computer under his arm. "I saw the article in the paper."

"You and everybody else."

"I know a little about this subject. I just wanted to let you know that some of your data is inaccurate."

"Data?" I asked, brushing my hair away from my eyes. "What data?"

"Well, you said that the earth had warmed up ten degrees in the twentieth century. In fact, it was just one degree. Still a very significant number, but much less than what you said."

It had been a long day. I wasn't in any mood to argue over how many degrees the earth had warmed up.

"Who cares?"

"It's just that if you're going to be quoted in newspapers, you want to be giving out accurate data. If somebody were to dispute your data and show you've got your facts wrong, it wouldn't help your cause any."

"Cause? I don't have any cause."

"Don't you want to preserve the planet for future generations?" he asked.

"Look," I told him, "I just want to make it through middle school."

"Hey, I'm just trying to help," Jess said as he walked away.

CHAPTER 6

Boys Will Be Boys

Most of the other kids at school, I suppose, hang out at the mall at night or at one of the pizza places in town. I go to the bookstore.

There's this big bookstore about five blocks from my house. It's open until ten o'clock. They have these nice comfortable chairs there, and nobody bothers you even if you don't buy anything. They also have books on just about any topic imaginable. I figured they had to have a book that would teach me how to kick a soccer ball.

I asked at the information desk where the Sports section was, because I'd never been there before. The various sports were in alphabetical order and it wasn't hard to find the section on soccer.

Soccer for Dummies. The Complete Idiot's Guide to

Soccer. Don't Know Nothin' 'bout . . . Soccer! Soccer for the Total Moron.

Man, didn't they have any books for people with a *brain*? I pulled *Soccer for the Total Moron* off the shelf.

It was a little embarrassing to be seen reading *any* soccer book. If any of my classmates came in and saw me reading *Soccer for the Total Moron*, I knew that I'd be the laughingstock of the school the next day. Not that any of the NASCAR idiots would be caught dead in a bookstore, of course.

Just to be on the safe side, I looked around for a bigger book to hide the soccer book in. The Art section was next to Sports. *The History of Modern Art* was the biggest and fattest book on the shelf, so I grabbed it, and sat down in one of the big chairs. I opened *The History of Modern Art* to the middle. Before slipping the soccer book inside it, my eye was caught by a large photo of an iron—the kind of iron you smooth clothes with—with metal spikes sticking out the bottom.

Whoa. I'd never seen anything like *that* before. Spikes sticking out of an iron? That made the iron into the exact opposite of itself. Cool. I turned the page. There were smaller photos—a bicycle mounted upside down on a stool. A snow shovel hanging on the wall of a museum. The *Mona Lisa* with a mustache. A *urinal*.

Somebody had actually put a *urinal* in a museum and called it art! It was very weird. And very cool. The caption under the pictures said the artist was a French guy named Marcel Duchamp and he created all this weird art in the 1920s.

I had been to a couple of museums with my parents when I was little, but found them to be boring. To me, "art" meant paintings of naked women and old dead guys. *This* was something completely different.

I could have looked at the book all night. Unfortunately, I had work to do. I slipped *Soccer for the Total Moron* inside the art book and turned to the first page. . . .

You say you're a total moron when it comes to soccer? Well, we're here to take you by the hand. You can't use your hands in soccer, so you won't be needing them. Ha-ha-ha. Just a little soccer humor there. But seriously, soccer is the universal sport. It is the most popular sport in the world. By the way, the rest of the world calls the game

"football." But for the purposes of this book, we're going to call it soccer. Soccer is simple to learn but difficult to master, but by the time you finish this book—

What a bore! I was having a tough time keeping my eyelids open. I flipped a few pages to the next chapter. . . .

In 1697, the emperor of China, Huang-ti, invented a game he called *tsu-chu*. It was played with a leather ball and players kicked it around with their feet. Sounds a lot like today's soccer, huh? But soccer was around long before that. Variations of the game were played in ancient Greece and Rome. And in some tribal societies, when the warriors wanted to have some fun, they would kick the severed heads of their rivals back and forth.

Oh, great. This was really a sport I wanted to be involved in!

The book was so boring, I thought I might slide right off the chair. I decided to skip all the introductory information and go straight to the part that I needed to know—how to kick the ball.

What is most important is that the inside of your foot must remain square, and by square we mean parallel to the target. The toe should be slightly higher than your heel. The ankle should be locked. Your knee is over the ball. Point your nonkicking foot, or planting foot, at the target and behind the plane of the ball. Point your kicking foot down and in . . .

I thought, would it be so terrible if I just let my eyes close for a minute or two? I was sure that if I rested my eyes briefly, I'd have enough energy when my eyes opened to finish reading this fascinating material.

Needless to say, I fell asleep instantly.

Some people remember their dreams vividly. I don't. The only time I remember a dream is when I take a nap in a strange place or at an unusual time. Like in a bookstore, after dinner.

I dreamed that I was in a jungle somewhere, drowning in quicksand. I didn't know how I got there, but I was almost completely buried. As my body sank lower and lower into the quicksand, insects began to land on my head. I couldn't raise my hands to swat them away. I tried to scream for help but no words came out of my mouth. I was helpless. My face was about to slip into the ooze.

At that moment, I heard a voice.

"Whisper . . ." the voice said softly. "Whisper."

My heart was racing. I opened my eyes. Jess Kirby, the science geek from school, was standing over me.

"I'm sorry to wake you up," he said, "but they just made an announcement that the bookstore is going to close in fifteen minutes."

"Oh . . . thanks," I mumbled, shaking the sleep from my eyes. I looked around. Jess had his trusty laptop with him, as always. The store was nearly empty. The art history book had fallen to the floor next to me and *Soccer for the Total Moron* was open on my lap. There was no point in trying to hide it.

"So I guess you're learning how to play soccer, huh?" Jess asked.

"Yeah," I admitted, getting up. "Got to start somewhere."

I collected my things and paid for *Soccer for the Total Moron* at the cash register. Jess opened the door for me as we walked out of the store.

I could have said good-bye and walked home by

myself. But it was late, and I didn't feel entirely comfortable walking home in the dark alone. I didn't feel entirely comfortable walking alongside Jess, either.

We walked about a block in silence. It was really awkward, and I was almost relieved when Jess started talking about the environment. He said the 1990s had been the hottest decade in the last thousand years, and 1998 was the hottest year ever recorded. According to Jess, by the year 2100, temperatures will have risen another five to ten degrees if we keep burning fossil fuels and cutting down trees.

"These are facts," Jess told me. "They were all laughing at you in school, but this is serious stuff."

"Listen," I told Jess, "I'm sorry about what I said to you in the lunchroom. I was having a tough day."

"Forget it," he replied. "When I saw the front page of the paper, the first thing I thought of was how bad the other boys were going to give it to you. I get made fun of all the time. But you're probably not used to being ridiculed so much."

"Jess, I get ridiculed and humiliated *constantly*."

"For what?" He seemed genuinely not to know.

"For not wearing the right clothes," I began.

"For my hair. For not being cool. For being different. For not taking gym. For being tall. For being fat. I could go on and on."

"You're not fat," he said.

"That's nice of you to say, but I am."

"Do you know that sixty percent of thirteen-year-old girls think they're overweight, while only twenty percent really *are* overweight?"

"How do you know that?" I asked. "*Why* do you know that?"

"I collect interesting facts," he said, patting his computer. "It's a hobby of mine."

"That's kind of a weird hobby."

"I don't think so," Jess replied. "Didn't you ever collect anything?"

"Mr. Peanut toys," I admitted.

"And you think *I'm* weird?" Jess chuckled. "Why do you care what anybody says about you, anyway? What difference does it make?"

"I don't know. I just care. I want to be liked. Don't you care what kids at school say about you?"

"No," he replied immediately. "They're not going to like me no matter what I say or do. I'm a nerd, a geek, a loser to them. So what? They're stupid. In a little more than a year, I'll be finished with middle school. In high school and college, the kids like *me* become the winners and those jerks who make fun of me now will be the losers. Just watch. Ten years from now I'll have my own company and they'll be working for me."

I shook my head. He seemed so sure of himself. How could Jess Kirby, a total nerd who gets made fun of just as much as I do, be filled with so much confidence? I'd bet if he were a girl, he wouldn't have that kind of confidence.

It's different for girls. If we're good-looking, they call us "dumb." If we get good grades, they call us "brain." If we speak our minds or act like guys, they call us "tomboy."

Then it occurred to me. Jess Kirby was just another boy. It wasn't that he was confident. He didn't have his whole career planned out in advance. This was just his way of putting the moves on girls.

He's not different from any other teenage boy, I realized. This was just his way to get me alone. He goes to the bookstore to meet girls instead of going to the mall. He spouts his facts and statistics to make you see how smart he is.

How could I have been so stupid? I was alone

and in the dark with a boy I hardly knew. I crossed my arms over my chest. We had reached my house. I stopped.

"Well, thanks again . . . for waking me up and stuff."

"No problem," Jess said.

I was in panic mode, but I tried not to show it. What if he tried to kiss me? Should I kiss him back? Maybe I *should*. It's not like anybody else was ever going to kiss me.

I wasn't used to this. It took me by surprise. I hadn't had any time to prepare. I was all mixed up.

"Well, I'll see you around school, I guess," Jess said, and he walked away.

I think I was a little disappointed.

CHAPTER 7

The Lesson

Some things you can learn from books. Some things you can't. You can learn how to cook a meat loaf or stir-fry chicken with a recipe book. You can learn all about the Civil War by reading a history book. But you can't learn how to play soccer by reading a soccer book. I know from experience.

When I got home from the bookstore, I went up to my room, put on my pj's, and got into bed with *Soccer for the Total Moron*. I turned off the light and used a flashlight just in case my nosy little sister was still awake in her room across the hall.

I opened the book and turned directly to the chapter on kicking penalty shots. I'm an intelligent person, I told myself. I can figure this out. How difficult can it be to kick a stupid ball twenty yards into a net?

I started reading.

In five minutes I was asleep.

The next morning, Saturday morning, I got up early. I slipped *Soccer for the Total Moron* under my mattress and went out to the garage. If I was going to learn how to kick a soccer ball, I would have to *kick* a soccer ball.

There's barely room in our garage for the car. The garage is almost completely filled with Briana's bats, balls, gloves, racquets, clubs, cleats, helmets, pads, paddles, and some other sports junk that I can't even identify. We call it "The Briana Nelson Hall of Fame."

A few of Briana's soccer balls were scattered around. I picked one up. It had been years since I had held a soccer ball in my hands. It felt heavy and bumpy. I was expecting it to be much lighter.

I was examining the ball when I sensed somebody standing behind me. I thought it might be a homocidal maniac, but it was just Briana.

"What are you doing in here?" she asked. "You never come in the garage."

"What, is this your personal space?"

I'm not quite sure why I was slinking around, hiding the soccer book and trying to avoid letting anyone see me practice. I guess I didn't want to make a fool of myself.

That's the way I am. I never like people looking at me. My attitude is that if nobody looks at me, nobody will ever see me do anything stupid. And if they never see me do anything stupid, they won't make fun of me. So, if I never do anything, nobody will ever make fun of me.

That's just a theory, of course. I'm not a shrink or anything.

"I'll teach you how to kick if you want," Briana offered.

When Briana was four, I taught her how to tie her shoes. When she was five, I taught her how to ride a bike. When she was six, I taught her how to read. I felt funny letting my little sister teach me how to do *anything*. But I had to admit Briana was a good player, so I swallowed my pride and agreed to let her give me a lesson.

She took the ball and paced off twenty yards from the garage door, where she drew an X mark on the driveway with a rock. Briana said our garage door is almost the exact same size as a soccer goal. She placed the ball on the X and scampered back to the garage.

"Go ahead," she challenged. "Try and kick one past me."

I went over and stood next to the ball.

"No, no, no!" Briana shouted. "If you want to kick it hard, you've got to take a running start."

I stepped back about ten feet and ran at the ball. When the moment seemed right, I brought back my leg and kicked.

I must have done something wrong, because my toe hit the ground a few inches before it hit the ball. My foot slammed into the driveway and I fell forward. The ball trickled a few feet off to the side and into the bushes.

"Oww!" I moaned as the pain shot up my leg.

Briana slapped her forehead and doubled over, holding her stomach.

"Stop laughing!"

"I'm not laughing!" she said, hiding her face in her sleeve.

"You are, too!"

"Let me show you how to do it," she said, retrieving the ball. "Let's switch places."

She took the ball back to the X mark on the

driveway. I limped over to the garage door. She took a few steps back from the ball.

"All you've got to do is whack it," she said as she ran forward. "Like this."

Her foot slammed into the ball and launched it. The ball was coming directly at my head. Instinctively, I put my hands over my face and ducked. I got my head out of the way, but the ball caught the end of my middle finger. It bent back so far I thought it was going to break off. The ball zoomed into the garage.

"Goooaaallllll!"

"Owwwww!" I screamed, holding my hand.

"A good keeper will block that shot," Briana said. "I didn't even kick it as hard as I could have."

"You did that on purpose!" I shouted. "You're still mad because I won the contest!"

"That's baloney," she insisted. "You just can't handle having a ten-year-old teach you how to do something."

"You don't just say 'whack it,'" I shouted back. "That's no way to teach somebody."

"Sor-ry!" Briana said, in a voice that indicated she wasn't sorry at all.

We were both partly right, I suppose. After our

hissy fit, we both stalked away. Clearly, Briana wasn't able or willing to teach me how to kick a soccer ball.

I didn't know where to turn next. My dad was in the Philippines or someplace like that until Tuesday. I didn't want to ask my mom for help. Being wheelchair-bound pretty much ruled her out anyway.

I was stewing in my room that afternoon when my mom rolled to the doorway.

"May I come in?" she asked quietly.

I had told her that I didn't want her barging into my room all the time without permission. She approached cautiously, like a lion tamer. I had trained her well.

"I guess so."

"You seem sadder than a gnat in a hailstorm, Whisper."

"I'm fine."

"Are you worried about this Million Dollar Kick thing?"

"No," I lied.

"You don't have to do it, you know. Nobody's forcing you to take that kick."

She knew I was lying about not being worried. My mother was always good at seeing right through me.

"I know I don't have to take the kick," I replied.

"So why do it? You don't care about money."

No way was I going to tell her that I had overheard her and dad saying what a loser I was through the vent in the wall. If she knew I could hear through the vent, she might block it up.

"I don't know," I said. "I guess I want to prove I can do it."

Mom rolled closer to my bed.

"Whisper," she said, "I know you don't like to hear this—

"Probably not."

"But I wanted you to know how proud I am of you."

I looked up at her. I couldn't remember the last time my mother said she was proud of me.

"For what?"

"I was doing the laundry this morning, and when I pulled the sheet off your bed, a book fell out."

"*Soccer for the Total Moron?*"

"Yes."

"You're proud of me for reading *that*?"

"Whisper, I'm proud of you because you care. When you were little, you cared so much . . . about everything. Gymnastics and ballet class. You cared about school and your friends. You cared about your Mr. Peanut collection. Remember?"

"Yeah."

"But ever since you got to middle school, it seemed like you didn't care about anything anymore. You just mope around all the time, angry at the world. I think this contest may have given you something to care about. And if I can do anything, *anything* to help you, I hope you'll ask me."

I wasn't going to get all choked up, no matter *what* she said. Mom told me she had something for me, and she rolled into her bedroom to get it. She came back out a minute or so later with a shoe box on her lap. She opened it and took out a pair of soccer cleats. They looked like they had never been worn.

"These were up in the attic," she explained. "They were mine when I was a teenager. Grandma bought them for me, but when I tried out for the soccer team, they told me girls weren't allowed to play. So I never had the chance to use them. I thought I would have to wait until Briana was big enough for them. But I think they're just the right size for you."

I wrapped my arms around her and let her hug me, partly because I wanted to and partly because I didn't want to let her see me cry.

"It doesn't matter if you make the goal or not," she whispered in my ear. "I'm just happy that you want to try."

CHAPTER 8

Head Games

The offices of the Oklahoma City Kick are inside their stadium, which is at 23rd Street and May Avenue. Briana had been to plenty of games at Taft Stadium. She was all excited when I was asked to appear at a press conference to promote the Million Dollar Kick, and I told her that she could come along.

"Do I have to get up on a stage?" I complained in the car on our way to the stadium.

"I'll get up on stage!" Briana chirped.

"You be nice, Whisper," my dad warned. "I expect no snotty remarks. Remember, this will be on *television*."

He said it like that was a *good* thing! It's bad enough to make a fool of yourself in front of a few kids at school. Making a fool of myself in front of millions of people watching TV would be even more humiliating.

We were met at the stadium by a lady who handed me a hideous blue-green-and-yellow jersey I had to wear over my shirt. On the front were the words OKLAHOMA CITY. On the back were the words DONUT CITY, with a big number one and six xeroes in the shape of doughnuts. Briana said it looked cool.

"I look like a walking lollipop," I moaned, after putting the jersey on.

As they led us into the ballroom where the press conference was to take place, I was so nervous I was shaking. The place was filled with reporters, many of them with cameras. A big banner on the wall announced THE KICK KICK BUTT! One of the big shots who run the team introduced himself to me, and then he climbed up on the stage.

"Ladies and gentlemen of the press," he announced, "as many of you already know, the Kick and Donut City are teaming up for a special event on June fifth. On that day, one lucky fan will get the chance to kick a twenty-yard shot worth a million dollars. That's a lot of doughnuts!"

A few people chuckled.

"We thought you might want to meet the lucky fan who will attempt that kick, along with the goalkeeper who will be trying her best to stop it. I'd like to introduce Whisper Nelson, and the star of the Oklahoma City Kick for the last six years, Carmen Applegate!"

Everybody started clapping. Briana gave me a shove forward, and I went up on the stage. Carmen Applegate came up from the other side of the room. She was tall and thin, with short brown hair. Probably in her thirties. Her jersey matched mine. The guy who had introduced us left the stage.

Carmen shook hands with me, and the photographers snapped pictures. She put her arm around my shoulder, and more pictures were taken. Carmen seemed perfectly comfortable up on the stage. There were so many camera flashes, I thought I might go blind.

"You look as nervous as a long-tailed cat on a porch full of rocking chairs," Carmen whispered in my ear.

"I am."

"Don't worry. Reporters don't bite."

I looked for my family in the audience. When I

made eye contact with them, they gave me the thumbs-up sign.

When the applause had died down, Carmen leaned toward the microphone. "Thank you," she said, "As a longtime member of the Kick, I just want to say what a pleasure it is for me to participate in this event. Soccer has been my life since long before I was Whisper's age. It's a dream come true for me to be playing the game professionally and my hope is that all the young girls of the Oklahoma City area follow their dreams, too. Whisper, do you have anything to add?"

"Uh, no," I said.

"Can't hear you!" somebody in the back shouted.

"Don't whisper, Whisper!" somebody else yelled, to everyone's amusement.

"I don't have anything to add," I squeaked into the microphone.

"A woman of few words," Carmen said. "I like that. Why don't we open up the floor to questions? And if the floor doesn't have questions, we can take some from you media folks."

A bunch of reporters raised their hands, and Carmen pointed to one of them.

"Carmen, why did you agree to be part of the

Million Dollar Kick?" the reporter asked. "It seems like a no-win situation for you. If you block Whisper's shot, everybody will say she's just a kid. And if you don't block it, you'll look bad."

"Actually, *everybody* wins," Carmen replied. "My goal is to help the sport of professional women's soccer grow. We want people to pay attention to our game. So anything that will get people to watch us is just fine with me. Girls like Whisper are the players and fans of tomorrow. If Whisper scores on me, I hope I'm mature enough to handle it."

"Carmen, how will you defend against Whisper?" asked another reporter.

"I'm going to treat Whisper just like any other opponent," she said, looking at me. "She's a big, strong girl, and it looks like she can kick a ball pretty hard. Blocking a twenty-yard kick with no defense, in my mind, is one of the most challenging plays for a goalkeeper to make. With a little luck, I'll stop her shot."

"Aren't you tempted to let the ball go through," somebody asked, "so Whisper can win the million dollars?"

"No, sir," Carmen replied. "If you've seen me

play, you know I'm a competitor. Even in an exhibition game, I don't like to lose. Whisper and I can hug and be all friendly up here on the stage. But once we get on the field, she is my opponent and I am hers."

"Whisper, do you have some secret strategy that you'll be using to score the goal on Carmen?"

Strategy?

I had no idea about strategy. I didn't even know there *were* strategies. I just thought you kicked the ball and hoped it went in the net.

"I'm just going to do my best," I said.

Carmen leaned into the microphone. "Smart girl," she said with a smile. "You didn't think Whisper was going to give away her strategy with me standing right here, did you?"

"How did you get the name Whisper?" somebody in the back hollered.

"I guess I don't talk very loud," I said.

"Can't hear you!" somebody screamed.

"I think that answers your question," Carmen quipped, and everyone laughed.

"Whisper, is it true that you haven't played soccer since you were in fourth grade?"

"Third, actually."

"How will you prepare for the shot, Whisper?"

"I guess I'll start by learning how to kick a soccer ball."

"Does Carmen have any weakness you might be able to take advantage of?"

"Oh, no," I said. "I don't think so. I'm sure she's a great goalie. I mean, keeper."

"Whisper, what will you buy with the million bucks if you score?"

"I'll just put it in the bank, I guess."

"Will either of you make a prediction?"

"I'm going to stop the shot," Carmen proclaimed.

"Whisper, how about you?"

"Uh . . . Carmen's going to stop the shot."

"*Booooo!*"

I looked around, surprised. The Donut City people were slapping their foreheads. I realized that I must have broken one of those silly unwritten sports etiquette rules. Apparently, athletes were not allowed to admit they think they're going to lose.

"I mean," I corrected myself, "I'm going to score."

"*Yaaaayy!*"

When it was all over, Carmen and I posed for more photos and she signed a picture of herself for me. Above her signature, she wrote, *To Whisper—Shoot for your goal.*

"Don't tell anyone," Carmen whispered in my ear as she signed the photo, "but this is going to be my last season with the Kick."

"Why?"

"They think I'm too old," she whispered. "If you score on me, they're going to use it as an excuse to fire me."

"You really think so?"

"Oh, I know so."

"That's not fair."

"Yeah, tell me about it. I've got two kids to support and no husband."

"You mean doing this Million Dollar Kick wasn't your idea?"

"No way," she muttered under her breath. "I would be crazy to agree to this stunt. But if I had refused, they would have fired me quick as a hiccup."

I wasn't going to mention what Carmen had said, but in the car on the way home my mother asked what Carmen had been whispering to me up on the stage. When I told them what Carmen said about getting fired if I scored on her, all three of them burst out laughing.

"What's so funny?" I demanded.

"She's trying to psych you out!" Briana announced. Mom and Dad agreed.

"What are you talking about?"

"She wants you to feel sorry for her," my father explained. "Athletes do this all the time. It's a head game. She's trying to get you to ease up, not try so hard, miss the kick."

"You're all crazy!" I said. "She's a professional soccer player. Why would she bother trying to psych me out?"

"It's obvious," Briana said. "She's scared of you."

CHAPTER 9

Take Your Business Elsewhere

About a mile from home is Rogers High School, where I'll go after next year. Rogers is a huge school, with over a thousand students. My mother suggested we drive over there after school and talk to the coach of the soccer team.

After getting lost in the winding hallways of Rogers for a few minutes, we finally found a door with a sign over it that said MRS. LORI BRADLEY, GIRLS' SOCCER.

Coach Bradley was having a heated discussion on the phone when we came into her office. Mom rolled her wheelchair up to the desk. Coach Bradley motioned for me to sit down until she was off the phone.

There were team photos and plaques all over the walls: OKLAHOMA STATE CHAMPIONS 1994.

OKLAHOMA STATE CHAMPIONS 1997. OKLAHOMA STATE CHAMPIONS 1998. OKLAHOMA STATE CHAMPIONS 2000.

"I don't care how much money you'll save!" Coach Bradley barked into the phone. "It's too dangerous! What are you going to say to the parents when their daughter tears up her knee and has to have an operation?"

Coach Bradley didn't like the answer she got and slammed down the phone.

"I'm sorry you all had to hear that," she told us, taking a sip from a bottle of water. "The Board of Ed is driving me crazy."

"What are they doing?" Mom asked.

"They're going to tear the grass off our field after this season and replace it with artificial turf."

"That's bad for the environment," I commented.

"Yup. Plus, more kids get injured on fake grass," the coach explained. "That stuff is murder on the legs."

"Is there anything you can do?" Mom asked.

"I have no say in the matter—budget cuts, and all that. It costs too much money to maintain real grass. That's what they tell me, anyways."

"But you've got the best team in the state," I protested.

"The Board of Ed doesn't care about how many games we win. They care about the bottom line," Coach Bradley said. "But that's *my* agitation. What can I do for you folks?"

"My name is Brenda Nelson," Mom said, extending a hand to shake, "and this is my daughter Whisper."

"Oh yeah, I remember the name. Not many girls around here named Whisper. I read about you in the paper. You won that contest."

"That's right." Mom smiled. "Mrs. Bradley, several people told me you are an excellent coach, and I was wondering if you would be able to help Whisper prepare for her kick."

"I'm sorry, ma'am. I don't do individual coaching."

"I don't expect you to work for free, Mrs. Bradley," Mom said, taking out her checkbook. "I'm prepared to pay whatever the going rate is. . . ."

"I wish I could help you, Mrs. Nelson," the coach replied. "But you must understand. I've got fifteen girls on my team who have been playing soccer since they were no bigger than a fire hydrant. They've devoted their lives to the game. No offense to Whisper, but it wouldn't be fair to them if I took time away from the team to coach a girl who doesn't even *like* soccer. I'm sorry."

It wasn't the nicest thing in the world to say, but I couldn't argue with her. Mom put her hand on mine.

"I understand," my mother sighed, unlocking the wheels of her chair. That's my mother's signal that it's time to go. "Can you suggest anyone else who might be able to help Whisper?"

The coach thought for a moment and looked at me. "Practice ends at six o'clock most weekdays," she said. "Why don't you come around then and ask the girls on the team? One of them might want to earn some extra money by coaching in her spare time."

"Thank you," Mom said. "We'll try that."

"Good luck with the kick," the coach said as I stood in the doorway. "You know, Carmen Applegate used to go to this school. She played for me years ago."

"What was she like?" I asked as the coach showed me a team picture on the wall with Carmen Applegate in it.

"Carmen was kind of a strange girl, but a great goalkeeper. She was crafty, and she'd do anything to win. A real competitor."

* * *

Mom made me an early dinner, and at five-thirty I rode my bike over to the athletic field behind the high school. Coach Bradley was in the middle of the field, running her players through a drill. Two rows of cones were lined up, and the players had been broken up into two groups. When Coach Bradley blew her whistle, two players would race each other to see which one could dribble the ball through her cones the fastest.

I watched from the distance for a few minutes. The players moved so gracefully and effortlessly, the way they could weave back and forth controlling the ball as if it were attached to their feet. It was like watching a ballet. Even though soccer— like all sports—still seemed utterly pointless to me, I couldn't deny their talent. I could never do anything like that. I was in awe of their ability.

Every so often one of the girls messed up and they'd all collapse into giggles. They seemed to be having so much fun together. I wish I had a group of friends to laugh and have fun with. As I watched them play, it struck me that their world was so different from mine.

Coach Bradley blew her whistle and all the girls

gathered around. They listened to her talk for a few minutes, then let out a loud *whoop* and clapped their hands. They scattered to the sideline to gather their equipment.

Cautiously, I rode my bike down to the sideline. I had been rehearsing in my mind, but I still wasn't sure what I was going to say. A group of the players were sitting on the bench changing into sneakers and talking among themselves. I stood there awkwardly for a minute or two before they noticed me. A few of them whispered to each other.

"What can we do for you?" one of the girls finally asked.

"Excuse me," I said nervously. "I was wondering if anybody does coaching in their spare time . . . for money."

They all stared at me.

"Not me," a tall girl with brown hair mumbled.

"Sorry, not interested," said the girl sitting beside her.

"I do," a thin black girl declared, standing up and stepping forward. "But I won't coach *you.*"

A few of the girls on the bench snickered. I took a step back. This wasn't going well. I wasn't expecting them to act hostile toward me.

"We heard about you," a blond girl with a pony-taii told me. "We figured you might be coming around. Did you really think we would help you after you said in the newspaper that our game is moronic? I mean, how moronic is *that*?"

"I . . ." I had no answer.

"She's gonna cry," the black girl told the others.

"Better take your business elsewhere," one of them advised me.

"I'm sorry," was all I said. Retreating quickly, I got on my bike and pedaled out of there. I left fighting back tears.

As I pedaled my bike home, I came to a decision. I didn't care about the million dollars. I didn't want to be famous. I didn't like the attention. I didn't like soccer. And I sure didn't need this aggravation.

I decided to back out of the Million Dollar Kick.

CHAPTER 10

Virtual Whisper and Virtual Carmen

When I got home from the soccer field, I went straight upstairs. I didn't feel like explaining to Mom and Briana that the girls on the high school soccer team had been mean to me. It had been my own fault, too. I was the one who said those dumb things to the reporter.

We have a phone in the hallway, and I dialed the number for Joe Fine, the guy who had informed me I'd won the Million Dollar Kick Contest.

"The offices of the promotion department are closed for the day," a computer voice droned. "We are open Monday through Friday from the hours of—"

I hung up. I would have to wait until the morning to tell Mr. Fine that he'd have to find someone else to take the Million Dollar Kick. I went into my room and started doing my homework.

Soon there was a knock on the door downstairs. One of Briana's perky little pals, I figured.

But then Briana came charging up the steps and pounding excitedly on my bedroom door.

"It's for *you*," she gushed. "It's a *boy*!"

"Very funny." The last time a boy came over to see me, I was in second grade and some of my friends were boys.

"For real!" Briana insisted.

"What does he look like?" I asked skeptically.

"He's got curly dark hair that's sort of messed up," Briana said. "And he's wearing sort of dorky clothes . . . and he's carrying a portable computer or something."

"That's Jess Kirby."

"Well, he wants to talk with you!" Briana bubbled. "Quick, comb your hair! Fix yourself up nice!"

"Oh, shut up."

I went downstairs, where Mom was hovering around Jess Kirby as if the Pope had come to visit. She had already given him apple juice, and she was practically force-feeding him her homemade cookies. It was like she had never seen a boy before. I was afraid that she might chain him to the kitchen table to make sure he didn't get away.

"I hope I'm not interrupting anything," Jess said when he saw me come downstairs.

"It's no interruption," Briana told him. "It's not like Whisper has anything else to do."

"Briana," I suggested. "Why don't you go play with your toys? In the middle of the street, preferably. Jess, please excuse my little sister. We found her on the front doorstep one day. We have no idea where she came from."

Briana stuck out her tongue at me and made kissy faces before running upstairs in a wave of giggles. Mom took the hint and had already scooted into the dining room. I had no doubt that both of them had their ears to the wall, listening to every word Jess and I said.

"I tried to call," Jess told me, "but your number is unlisted. So I thought I'd just come over."

"It's no problem," I said, doing my best to act like boys came over to see me all the time. "What's up?"

"Well," Jess said. "I was thinking about you."

I caught my breath so he wouldn't hear me gasp. I couldn't imagine that any boy had ever thought about me, except maybe to think of a new way to torture me for his own amusement.

"I was thinking about that million dollar kick you're going to take," he added.

Oh.

Jess put his laptop on the table, opened it, and pushed a key to make the screen light up. There was a line drawing of a soccer goal on the screen.

"Are you into soccer?" I asked.

"No," he said, fussing with the keyboard. "I played once when I was little, but my glasses fell off when some kid bumped into me, and some other kid stepped on them with his cleats and crushed them. That was enough soccer for me. But I think I figured something out that may be useful to you."

This I had to see.

"A soccer goal is exactly eight feet high and twenty-four feet across," Jess explained. "I looked it up. That's one-hundred and ninety-two square feet, which is a lot of area for a goalie to cover. The ball itself is only twenty-seven inches in circumference."

"Um-hmm?"

"Carmen Applegate is five feet, eight inches tall," he continued. "She weighs one-hundred and twenty-five pounds. I estimate a woman of that height and weight can jump—at best—two and a half feet in any direction. She is also right-handed, so she can probably jump farther and better to her right side than she can to her left side."

"How do you know so much about Carmen Applegate?"

"Oh, you'd be surprised how much you can find out about people on the Internet," Jess replied, a twinkle in his eye. "There's no personal privacy anymore. Now watch this . . ."

He clicked a few keys and a stick figure appeared in the middle of the goal.

"That's Carmen Applegate," Jess pointed out. He clicked some more keys and another stick figure appeared, this one on the field. "And this is you."

"I lost some weight," I cracked, but Jess was too

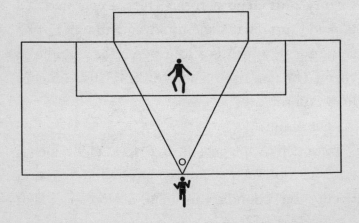

involved with the computer to notice.

"In this simulation," Jess continued, "I can make Virtual Whisper kick the ball to any location and at any speed up to one-hundred miles per hour. The computer will tell us if Virtual Carmen will be able to block the shot or not. You see, it's all physics."

"Cool!"

I had to admit, Jess was a genius. No wonder he was so sure he would be running his own company in ten years.

"See what happens if I kick the ball right at her," I said.

Jess tapped a few keys, and Virtual Whisper kicked the ball right up the middle, at fifty miles per hour. It hit Virtual Carmen and bounced away. When he increased the speed to seventy miles per hour, she still blocked the shot.

"Even if you kicked it one-hundred miles per hour," Jess explained, "you can't score a goal if you kick it up the middle. And no human being can kick a soccer ball one-hundred miles an hour."

"What happens if I aim for the sides of the goal?" I asked.

"No problem," Jess said, playing with the keys. He had Virtual Whisper kick the ball two feet to the left, at sixty miles per hour. Virtual Carmen moved over and blocked the shot. When the ball was kicked two feet to the right, the same thing happened.

"How far over do I have to kick the ball for Virtual Carmen to miss?" I wondered out loud.

"Let's see."

Jess had Virtual Whisper kick the ball over and over again, each time a little closer to the sides of the goal. What he discovered was that Virtual Carmen could not stop a fifty-mile-per-hour shot if it was placed either four and a half feet to her left or five feet to her right.

"That's because she's right-handed," Jess explained.

"That's amazing!" I said.

"There's more," Jess said, clearly proud of his simulation. "Watch this."

He made a series of kicks, this time changing the height of the ball as it crossed the goal line. If Virtual Whisper kicked the ball at waist height, Virtual Carmen would stop it seventy percent of the time. But if the ball was kicked higher or lower, Virtual Carmen was not as good at stopping it, especially as the speed of the ball was increased.

"So this is what I figured out," Jess said. "If you can kick the ball within two feet of the right post, either on the ground or up in the corner, it is impossible for Carmen Applegate to block the shot. That is, of course, assuming you kick it sixty miles per hour or faster."

"Impossible?" I asked.

"*Impossible*," Jess repeated, sitting back, satisfied that he had proved his point. "A taller goalie might be able to block that kick, but not Carmen Applegate. And remember, this is assuming that she does everything right. If she trips or stumbles or jumps to the wrong side, you don't have to kick the ball that hard or that accurately."

I was impressed, not only by Jess's simulation, but also by the fact that he had bothered to create the simulation without getting paid, rewarded, or even asked to do it. He had to be either a genius, crazy, or maybe he *did* like me. Or maybe he just had too much time on his hands.

"You did this all by yourself?" I asked.

"Well, it's a very simple program," he explained modestly. "Once I plugged in the data, it was a simple matter to crunch the numbers. The computer did all the work, really."

"But why? Why did you do it?" I asked. I was trying my best to give Jess the chance to say that he liked me, or something even close to that.

"I enjoy intellectual exercises," he replied. "My interest in soccer is purely scientific. It allowed me to practice my computer skills."

Maybe he was telling the truth, and maybe he wasn't. Maybe he was thinking the same thing I was thinking. I was thinking that I liked him. But somehow, I couldn't make those words come out of my mouth.

"Well . . . I have to go," he said, after the awkward silence. He closed the computer without bothering to turn it off and backed toward the front door as if the house were on fire. "I hope that helped."

"Don't go!" I said, following him out the door to the porch. "I need to tell you something."

"What?" He looked frightened.

"I want you to know that I really appreciate all the work you put into the simulation," I told him. "But I've decided not to take the kick."

"What?!"

"Let's face it," I explained. "It doesn't matter what the computer says. I can't kick a soccer ball sixty miles per hour. I can't even kick a soccer ball *two* miles per hour. This afternoon I went over to the high school and asked some of the girls on the soccer team if they would coach me. They laughed in my face."

"Whisper, I can't believe you're saying this!" Jess no longer seemed like he was in a rush to leave. "Are you going to let a few jerks on the soccer team make up your mind for you? This kick is entirely makeable. You can *make* this shot. Even *I* could make this shot. *Anybody* could make this shot with a little practice."

"I know, but—"

"Your kick will be twenty yards, just eight yards behind the penalty spot. Do you have any idea of the percentage of penalty kicks that go in?"

"No."

"I looked it up," he informed me. "Seventy-five percent. Three out of every four penalty kicks make it past the goalie. So figuring that an amateur can't kick as hard as a professional soccer player, I still estimate you've got a fifty-fifty chance in making the goal. Fifty-fifty! For a million dollars! How can you pass that up? Do you know how much money you'd have in ten years if you invested a million dollars in some good stocks? I worked it out—"

"Jess, I don't care if it's *ten* million dollars. I just don't want to deal with it anymore. Ever since I won this stupid contest, everyone has been staring at me, making fun of me, humiliating me. You don't know what it's like."

"Oh, I know what it's like," Jess insisted. "You think I don't know what it's like to be made fun of? Everybody has been calling me a nerd and a geek since I was eight years old. The difference between me and you is that I don't care and you care too much."

"There's another difference," I pointed out. "You're a boy and I'm a girl. It's harder for girls."

"You think so, huh?" Jess laughed. "You think it's fun when every guy in the class plays sports but you can't throw or catch a ball? You think it's fun, always getting picked last in gym class? Or not being able to talk to anybody because all they want to talk about is some game they all watched on TV? Oh, that's *lots* of fun. Boys have it *soooo* easy."

Somehow, it never even occurred to me that boys went through problems growing up. I just figured they all cruised through life while girls were tormented. Maybe it was just the *dumb* boys who didn't seem to have any problems. They were too stupid to even know they *had* problems.

"I'm sorry."

"It's okay. Just do me one favor," Jess urged. "Don't make your decision about this kick just because some high school girls made fun of you. Take a day and think about what I showed you on the computer. Will you do that?"

"Okay," I agreed.

Jess was halfway down the street when I thought of something I needed to ask him. I ran outside and caught up with him.

"When you did that research about Carmen Applegate," I asked, "did it say anything about her personal life? Her family, and stuff?"

"Sure, but what difference does that make?"

"I was just wondering how many kids she has."

"Kids?" Jess stopped to think. "Carmen Applegate doesn't have any kids."

So she was lying to me! Briana was right. Carmen *was* trying to psych me out at the press conference. My little sister was smarter than I thought she was.

I gave Jess my phone number in case he ever had to call me again. As soon as I got back inside the house, Briana was all over me.

"He's really cute!" she giggled. "Did he ask you out?"

"Oh, be quiet."

CHAPTER 11

Opening My Eyes

I had promised Jess I would give it a day before deciding whether or not to drop out of the Million Dollar Kick Contest. By the time school was over, I still hadn't made up my mind. I was in my room working on my homework when there was a knock at the front door. Briana was over at a friend's house, so I got up to see who it was.

"Does Whisper Nelson live here?" I heard a female voice ask my mother.

The girl in the doorway was older than me, maybe fifteen or sixteen. She was wearing soccer shorts and a T-shirt, and her hair was pulled back into a ponytail with a thick orange rubber band.

"My name is Ellie Gonzales," she said politely. "You don't know me."

But I did recognize her. She was one of the girls

on the high school soccer team. While most of the other girls had been mean to me the previous day, this girl had remained quiet. Ellie told me she was a senior, and the starting goalkeeper.

"You sure are popular lately," Mom whispered to me as she went to get her usual assortment of cookies.

"I wanted to apologize for the way some of my teammates acted toward you yesterday," Ellie told me.

"It's okay."

"One of them had tacked the newspaper article about you up on the bulletin board in our locker room," Ellie continued. "The team made an agreement not to help you if you came around asking for a coach."

"Then why are *you* here?" I asked.

"To help you," she said. "If they won't coach you, I will."

Mom rolled back in with the cookies. I gave her a look to let her know this was a private conversation. She scooted back to the kitchen. Ellie selected a cookie and sat on the couch. I took a chair across from her.

"Why do you want to help me?" I asked.

"You remind me of me," Ellie replied, a hint of sympathy in her eyes. "When I was in seventh grade, I was the class dork. The boys called me unbelievable names. The girls didn't want to have anything to do with me. Being Hispanic didn't help any. I felt like I was a different species from everybody else. I felt like I was . . ."

"Whomperjawed?"

"Yeah, whomperjawed."

"I feel that way a lot."

"Middle school is the pits," Ellie continued. "I was bored and angry all the time. I hated everybody and everything."

"You don't seem that way now."

"A couple of things happened," Ellie said. "I grew up, for one thing. Physically and emotionally. It's easier to make friends in high school, too. But mostly it was because I found something I was really interested in—soccer."

"I can't see myself getting interested in soccer," I told her.

"It doesn't have to be soccer," Ellie replied. "It could be anything."

"Do you want to coach me because you feel sorry for me?" I asked bluntly.

"Listen," Ellie said, fixing her gaze on me, "I didn't come over here so you'd have a shoulder to cry on. But when I was in middle school, nobody ever came around to help me. Here I am. If you don't want my help, it's okay. But I'm offering."

"I *do* want your help."

"Okay, then. You've got about six weeks to get ready for the Million Dollar Kick."

"So what do I do next?" I asked.

"Stretching exercises," Ellie instructed. "Meet me at the high school tomorrow around three-fifteen."

"I'll be there."

I finished my homework early that night, so I decided to go to the bookstore. Partly, I went because I thought I might bump into Jess again. But also, ever since the last time I was there, I'd been thinking about those strange, disturbing pictures I had seen in the art book. I couldn't get them out of my mind.

An iron with spikes sticking out the bottom. The *Mona Lisa* with a mustache. A urinal. I wanted to look at them some more.

At the bookstore, Jess was nowhere to be found. It took a few minutes to find *The History of Modern*

Art again. Fortunately, nobody had bought the book. I grabbed it off the shelf. One of the comfortable chairs was empty, so I curled up in it. Flipping through the pages, I found the images again. The caption under the mustached Mona Lisa said . . .

The senseless death and destruction of World War I led to an artistic protest movement. Many artists, witnessing the horror of war firsthand, came to this conclusion: A civilization that created such killing did not deserve art. Their "anti-art" celebrated ugliness instead of beauty, nonsense instead of logic and reason. They coined a meaningless word to describe their work—"Dada."

Dada. What a wonderful word, I thought.

I was riveted by the images, and turned the page. My reward was an even more fascinating image.

It was a painting of a landscape. But instead of trees and rivers and flowers, there were three clocks. Not ordinary clocks. Drippy, misshapen clocks. Their faces were melting like Popsicles in the sun. One of the clocks was hanging over the branch of a dead tree. It was disturbing, and at the same time it was beautiful. It said under the picture that the artist's name was Salvador Dali.

I turned the page and there were other strange

paintings: a man with a giant apple hovering in front of his face. A locomotive coming out of . . . a fireplace! A pancake on a plate . . . with an eye in the middle of it!

The artist's name was René Magritte. His images looked like photographs, but they were paintings. They were pictures of things that could not exist in the real world. I had never seen anything like them. I began reading . . .

In the 1920s, Dada evolved into Surrealism. To surrealist artists, truth was found only in the subconscious, or hidden part of the mind. They believed fantasy and dreams could be joined with the real world to create an absolute reality, a "surreality." They expressed it in a new way, with fantastic, hallucinatory imagery.

I had never thought of art as anything but pretty pictures to cover bare walls. But this art made me think. I could relate to the anger of Dada. My life felt surreal sometimes. I felt like I had opened my eyes for the first time.

I dug out my wallet and found I had twenty-five dollars. Just enough to buy *The History of Modern Art*.

After I had paid for the book, something *really* surreal happened. There was a tap on my shoulder. Hoping it was Jess Kirby, I turned around with a smile on my face. But Jess wasn't there.

It was Carmen Applegate.

"Funny seeing you here, Whisper," she beamed. "I hope you've been practicing for your big kick."

"A little." I didn't trust her after what she had said to me at the press conference. The less she knew about me, the better.

"I wanted to give you a little tip," Carmen said, lowering her voice. "When you run up to the ball, don't be distracted by the gray background behind the goal. Sometimes it throws kickers off."

"Thank you," I replied.

How stupid did she think I was? Obviously, she had given me that little "tip" to psych me out.

"Any time," Carmen said. "If I can help you in any way, don't hesitate to ask."

"Sure," I said. "And if you ever need a baby-sitter, give me a call."

Carmen looked at me, puzzled for a moment.

"For those two young kids you told me you have," I explained, not sure if I had hidden my smirk adequately.

Carmen looked like she was trying to figure out

111

if I knew the truth or not. She must have decided that I did, because she burst into tears, burying her head in her elbow.

"I'm sorry I lied to you," she sobbed. "I don't have any children. It's just that I was so upset when I found out the Kick are trying to get rid of me, I said the first thing that came to my mind. You believe me, don't you, Whisper?"

"Yes," I lied. I didn't believe her for a moment. The tears were fake. Everything she said or did, I was beginning to think, was just another attempt to psych me out.

CHAPTER 12

The Genius of Jess Dada

The world of science hit a new low. My science teacher, Mr. McGrath, had offered extra credit for anyone who wanted to create an invention or experiment. He said he did it to give us a chance to improve our grade before the end of the term.

I knew I was going to get a B in science, and that was good enough for me. Not many kids took Mr. McGrath's offer. But Dan Mills did. The King of the NASCAR idiots was up at the front of the class showing off the brilliant experiment he had designed.

"In this-here jar, I have placed one cup of ordinary backyard dirt, right?" Dan explained, a smirk on his face for the benefit of his moronic friends. "And this other jar contains two tablespoons of plain old, ordinary tap water. Right?"

I glanced over at Jess Kirby, who was shaking his head from side to side, as if he was ashamed to be a member of the same species as Dan Mills.

"Observe what occurs when I combine these two substances together," Dan said, pouring the contents of one jar into the other.

We all watched as he mixed the solution with "an ordinary, everyday pencil."

"It makes mud!" Dan proclaimed. "A substance that, though sharing properties of both water and dirt, is completely different!"

Well, the NASCAR idiots must have thought Albert Einstein himself had come to pay a visit on the class. They were applauding, hooting, and hollering until Dan bowed modestly and held up his hands to calm down his loyal followers.

"He's a genius!" one of the NASCAR idiots declared. "That deserves the Cy Young Award or somethin'."

"So," Mr. McGrath said, his arms folded at his chest, "you discovered that by combining water and dirt you could create mud, is that it, Mr. Mills?"

"Sure 'nuff. Pretty awesome experiment, huh, Mr. McG?"

The NASCAR idiots high-fived Dan all the way to his seat.

"And what did you hope to prove by performing this experiment?" Mr. McGrath asked.

"I was hopin' to prove that you oughta give me a C instead of a D this term, Mr. McG."

Everybody laughed. I suspect half the class was laughing because Dan's experiment was so dumb, and the other half was laughing because he had made science look stupid right in front of Mr. McGrath.

"If I was the teacher, I'd give him an A," one of the NASCAR idiots suggested.

"The day you become a teacher, Mr. Conrad, I'm retiring," snorted Mr. McGrath. "Does anyone else have an experiment or invention to demonstrate for us?"

Jess Kirby raised his hand. I was sure he already had an A in science and didn't need any extra credit. Everybody knew Jess Kirby got straight As. He had probably done a science project just for the fun of it. Mr. McGrath called on Jess, who brought a funny-looking flashlight to the front of the room.

"I went to use this flashlight the other day," Jess said, "but the batteries were dead. I didn't have any batteries in the house. So I started to wonder if a different energy source could light the flashlight. I had a solar-powered calculator in my desk drawer and figured out how to hook up the solar panel to the flashlight. I think I have created the first solar-powered flashlight without batteries. See? It works!"

Everyone watched as Jess held the flashlight up and flipped on the button. It was weak, but the bulb did light up. A few "wows" and "ooos" were heard throughout the class.

"Wait a minute," Dan Mills said, not bothering to wait for Mr. McGrath to call on him. "That don't make no sense!"

"What do you mean, Mr. Mills?" asked Mr. McGrath.

"You use a flashlight to see in the dark, right? Well, solar power uses the sun, right? And the sun ain't out when it's dark, right? So what good is a solar-powered flashlight? Shoot, that's like the sorriest invention in the history of the world."

"He's right!" one of his NASCAR buddies agreed, high-fiving Dan Mills in honor of his scientific insight.

"Oh, like *your* experiment was so great?" one of the other boys said to Dan.

"At least you can *do* somethin' with mud," he shot back. "A solar-powered flashlight is about as useless as a one-legged man in a butt-kickin' contest."

"Yeah!"

"I never said it was useful," Jess explained quietly. "My interest was purely scien—"

"Dorkus!"

"Kirby the loser does it again!"

A lot of the kids were snickering. I couldn't take it anymore.

"He's not a loser!" I said, standing up. "He's an artist!"

"*Oooooooh!*"

"Whisper, do you care to explain?" Mr. McGrath asked.

"A solar-powered flashlight is a brilliant juxta-position of two objects that are incompatible in reality," I said. "What Jess has created is Dada art."

"Dada?" somebody asked.

"Juxta-who?"

"Don't you *get* it?" I asked. "It's playful. It's nonsense! He's poking fun. It's surrealistic!"

The whole class stared at me. Jess stared at me. He probably thought I was out of my mind, but he seemed relieved that somebody had defended him. I knew that nobody in the class had any idea what Dada or Surrealism were. Mr. McGrath, sensing he had lost control of the class, went to his desk to prepare for his next class.

"Whisper's in *lovvvvvvve*," Dan Mills announced. "Whisper loves Kirby."

"Kirby Dada."

"Dada and Dumdum."

"When they get married," one of the other NASCAR idiots cracked, "they'll probably light their house with solar-powered flashlights."

"Shut up!" I shouted. "How can the human race survive with so many people around who are dumber than dirt?"

The argument didn't continue, because at that moment, the school alarm rang out. It was one long, continuous clang, the signal in our school for a tornado drill.

Oklahoma, Texas, Kansas, and Nebraska are called "Tornado Alley," because we get hit by a lot of tornadoes for some reason. Fifty people were killed by a tornado that swept through Oklahoma City in 1999. I saw one once from a distance when I was a little girl, and it was terrifying.

"I hate those NASCAR idiots," I told Jess as we

filed out of the classroom. The room we were in had a wall of windows, and whenever there was a tornado drill we had to move to the safer rooms with fewer windows and get down low to the ground.

"Forget about them!" Jess replied. "It's not worth it. There's nothing you can do to make people like that like you."

"They make me crazy!"

"Don't let them bother you," he told me. "Focus on what's important. Like that soccer thing. Have you made up your mind yet? Are you going to take the shot or not?"

"I decided to take it."

"Good move."

A few minutes later, the alarm rang again, telling us it was safe to return to class.

After school I did some stretching exercises at home and rode my bike over to the high school. Ellie Gonzales had told me to meet her at the front office at three-fifteen, but she wasn't there yet so I took a seat on a bench. The school had already emptied out, but a few kids came in and walked by me. I wondered where they were going. There was

a small sign on the wall: ART CLUB MEETS 2:45
TODAY IN ROOM 101.

I peeked my head around the corner and saw
room 101. There were some kids in there, standing
behind easels. Some of them were working with
paintbrushes, others had pencils in their hands.

"You're welcome to come inside," somebody
behind me said. I turned around, a little surprised.
It was a lady wearing a smock, probably the art
teacher.

"I'm not a student here," I told her. "I go to the
middle school. I'm just waiting to meet someone."

"That's okay," she said. "Everybody's welcome."

She introduced herself as Mrs. Hatfield and said
the Art Club was for people who wanted to
express themselves creatively in any way they
liked. She showed me what the students were
working on. Besides the painters, there was a girl
sitting at a potter's wheel molding clay. One boy
was carving a giant piece of Styrofoam with a
razor blade. Another boy was holding a propane
torch, melting crayons and dribbling all the colors
together into a weirdly shaped sculpture.

"I call it *Self Portrait*," he said when he saw me
peering over his shoulder.

"It's very nice," I told him. He smiled and thanked me.

"Would you like to make something?" Mrs. Hatfield asked me.

"I really can't," I explained. "I need to meet somebody at three-fifteen."

"We're here every day," she said. "Y'all come back when you have more time."

"I will."

I rushed back to the front office and saw Ellie arriving, a big gym bag over her shoulder. I waved hi and she led me to her car, a little Subaru that looked like it must have had a million miles on it.

"Aren't you afraid one of your teammates might see you coaching me?" I asked.

"I thought about that," Ellie replied, turning the key in the ignition to make the car gurgle to life. "But then I decided that was silly. I'm a senior, it's April, and I'm about to graduate. It doesn't make any difference what my teammates think. And besides, where I'm taking you, nobody is going to see us."

"Where are you taking me?"

"Oh, you'll see," she said, hitting the gas and roaring out of the parking lot.

CHAPTER 13

Shooting Pool

Oklahoma City is not some hick town in the middle of nowhere. About a million people live here. The downtown area has a lot of big office buildings. When Ellie turned on to Walker Avenue in the heart of the city, I wondered where she was taking me. There weren't any soccer fields that I knew of downtown, except for Taft Stadium, where the Oklahoma City Kick play.

"How much do you know about soccer?" Ellie asked, as we waited for the light to change at Tenth Street.

"Not much," I replied. "I know you can't use your hands."

"But you know that the goalkeeper can, right?"

"Oh yeah," I giggled. "I forgot."

Ellie shook her head and grinned. To her, forgetting that a goalie can use her hands must have been like forgetting that the earth moves around the sun.

We drove east on Tenth Street past St. Anthony Hospital and turned south onto Robinson. In a couple of minutes we were at Fifth Street. There to the right was the Oklahoma Memorial, the site of the Oklahoma bombing, which was the worst act of terrorism ever on American soil.

On April 19, 1995, a guy named Timothy McVeigh set off a truck bomb in front of the Alfred P. Murrah Federal Building at that spot. The nine-story building collapsed; 168 people were killed, including nineteen kids at a day-care center on the second floor. It was a horrible tragedy.

After they cleared away all the debris, the site was turned into a memorial. Now it's a quiet park with 168 chairs on the grass, one for each person who died in the bombing. Big bronze slabs at the sides of the memorial say "9:01" and "9:03." The bomb went off at 9:02 that day.

As we drove around the block on Harvey Street, I could see a group of tourists looking solemnly at the fence where people have left notes, photos, and personal mementos honoring the victims of the blast. It has been years now, but people still come from all over the world to pay their respects.

I didn't know what Ellie had in mind. Where was she taking me? She turned onto Fifth Street and parked the car a block and a half away from the bomb site at the corner of Robinson Avenue. I looked up at the plain white building next to us. It was eight stories high and looked abandoned. There were lots of windows, but they were all boarded up.

A fence surrounded the building. It was about eight feet high and topped with barbed wire. Behind the fence I could read a sign: YMCA OF GREATER OKLAHOMA CITY.

"I used to play here when I was little," Ellie told me as she grabbed a gym bag out of the back seat and hopped out of the car.

"It looks like a mess now," I said, following her toward the fence.

"The windows were blown out in the bombing," she replied. "But I still love this place."

Ellie led me to a hole in the fence that was just big enough for us to squirm through. The doors were padlocked shut, so we didn't even try to get in that way. The first-floor windows of the building were high off the ground, but Ellie gave me a boost up so I could climb in. She managed to get up without any help.

The building was like an egg with everything scraped out but the shell. The only thing left inside was a big swimming pool. It had been drained, and Ellie climbed down the ladder to the bottom of the pool. There was still some debris scattered around.

"*This* is where we're going to practice?" I asked, my voice echoing off the walls. "Isn't it a little dangerous?"

"A little," she replied, taking two soccer balls out of her gym bag. "But we'll be careful."

"Why do you want to practice here?"

"Privacy, memories," Ellie said, walking over to the middle of the pool where the drain was. "Plus, you don't have to chase the ball. No matter where you kick it, it always comes back."

She whacked the ball off one of the sides of the pool. The floor sloped down slightly on all sides leading to the drain, so the ball rolled right back to her.

"First things first," Ellie announced. "That hair has got to go."

"You're going to cut it off?" I sputtered, covering my head with my hands.

"I'm going to get it off your face," she said, taking a rubber band out of her pocket. "You can't kick if you can't see."

"But my ears stick out," I protested. It was the first time I had ever told anyone that my hairstyle was determined solely by the size of my ears.

"They do not," Ellie scoffed, wrapping the rubber band around my hair.

"Ponytails make me look so . . . perky," I complained.

"A little perky wouldn't hurt you. Okay," Ellie said, clapping her hands. "Let's get started. Are you left- or right-handed?"

"Left."

"Me too. If you're left-handed, you're probably left-footed."

"I didn't even know you could be *any* footed."

"Oh, yeah," Ellie informed me. "If you're left-handed, the whole left side of your body is usually stronger than your right side. Let's do a little test."

She picked up a stone from the floor of the pool and tossed it about ten feet away.

"See that rock?" she said. "Stand here and tell

me which foot you'll use to kick it."

"How should I know until I get there?"

"Walk over to it and tap it with whichever foot feels more comfortable."

I walked up to the stone. When I got there, my left foot was in position to kick it. I didn't *try* to use my left foot, but it was just naturally there. Ellie retrieved the stone and tossed it in the other direction.

"Tap it again," she instructed.

I walked over to the stone and kicked it, again using my left foot. She did it one more time, and again I kicked the stone with my left foot.

"You weren't even aware of it," Ellie said, "but as you were approaching the rock, your brain made a calculation to adjust your stride slightly so that you would kick with your stronger foot."

"I guess I'm left-footed," I said.

"That's right. Now, do you know what part of your foot you use to kick the ball?"

It sounded like a stupid question. I went over to the ball and gave it a kick.

"Wrong," Ellie said immediately. "Your toe has a very small surface area. If you miss the center of the ball by a half an inch, your shot will miss the goal."

"So what am I supposed to kick with?"

"The *laces*," Ellie explained. "It's a bigger surface. In tennis, racquets have become bigger over the years. Golf clubs have become bigger, too. That's because a bigger hitting surface hits a ball harder and more accurately. It's the same in soccer."

I went over to the ball and kicked it with the laces.

"It feels weird," I told Ellie.

"You'll get used to it with practice," she replied. "As you kick, you want your toe pointed down and your ankle locked."

She smashed a ball at the side of the pool. The boom echoed off the walls of the YMCA. I tried the same thing and the ball dribbled pathetically to the wall.

"Good!" Ellie shouted. "Pay attention to your nonkicking foot. It should be even with the ball, maybe four inches away, and pointed toward your target. You want your body over the ball. As you kick, focus all your concentration on the ball. Don't lift your head, and don't look at your target. You should already know in your head where that is. Let your striking foot swing through the ball, and always follow through. If you want to give the ball some loft, at the instant of contact, lean back just a little."

Ellie demonstrated again. Then she pulled a piece of chalk from her pocket and drew two vertical lines eight yards apart on the wall of the pool. She pulled a little device out of her gym bag and put it on the ground. It was about the size of a Walkman.

"What's that?" I asked.

"It records the speed of the ball in miles per hour," Ellie explained. "I borrowed it from Coach Bradley."

"Cool."

"Go ahead," she commanded, as she placed the ball in the middle of the pool. "Kick a goal."

I ran up the ball and tried to kick it with the laces of my cleat, as Ellie had instructed. I had to turn my body sideways a little to do that, which was uncomfortable. My foot missed the ball completely and I almost fell down.

"Try again," Ellie said.

I noticed that she didn't laugh at me. Whenever I tried to throw or kick a ball with my sister Briana, she would laugh when I failed. It made me not want to try anymore.

I ran up to the ball again. This time I managed to get my foot on it, sending it trickling off to the left of the goal. Ellie showed me the speed on the meter—five m.p.h. I remembered that Jess had told me I would need to kick the ball at least sixty miles per hour to score a goal.

"Good," Ellie yelled. "Again."

I kicked the ball again. And again and again and again. Some of the kicks went straight and registered in the twenties on the meter. Some of them barely registered at all. A couple of times I hit the ball off the side of my foot. No matter what, Ellie kept shouting encouraging things and correcting my form.

After about an hour, Ellie decided I'd had enough for the day. We climbed out of the YMCA window and into her car.

"I was terrible," I pointed out as we headed back home.

"You were not," she insisted.

"You're just being nice."

"I am not."

"I'll never be ready in time for the Million Dollar Kick. It's five weeks from tomorrow. I'll make a fool of myself."

Ellie did not respond to that, and I got the message—she didn't want to hear negative comments.

"Here's your homework assignment," Ellie said as we pulled into my driveway. "Starting tonight and every day, I want you to kick a ball twenty yards against your garage door. Kick it a hundred times, fifty aimed at the left side and fifty aimed at the right side. Got it?"

"Okay," I agreed.

My mother was sitting on the front porch, and she waved as I got out of the car.

"You look good in a ponytail," Mom hollered. "How about some cold drinks, girls?"

"Thanks, but I've got to go to practice, Mrs. Nelson," Ellie shouted back.

"How did Whisper do?"

"She made progress," Ellie replied diplomatically.

But when you start from where I was starting, it was almost impossible to *avoid* making progress.

CHAPTER 14

Keeping Secrets

I took my hundred shots at the garage door, as Ellie told me to, being careful to use the correct kicking form. It was hard work and not a lot of fun, especially when I missed the garage door entirely and had to go chase the ball into our neighbor's yard.

When I woke up the next morning, I could barely lift my body out of bed. The muscles in my thighs and calves were killing me. My muscles were sore in places I didn't even know I *had* muscles. I felt like an old lady.

"It's called being out of shape," Briana told me cheerfully over breakfast.

"Just amputate my legs," I moaned, "and I'll be fine."

My mom gave me a couple of Advil, and I

struggled through school. During the course of the day my legs loosened up a little and I didn't feel as much soreness. That was a relief, because I had promised Ellie I'd meet her at the high school again at three-thirty. I got there early and went straight to the room where the Art Club meets. Only a few kids had arrived.

"You came back!" said Mrs. Hatfield. "I hoped you might. Would you like to create something today?"

"Sure thing!" I replied enthusiastically.

"Wonderful. What's your medium?"

I didn't know what she meant by the word "medium," so I just looked at her with what I'm sure was a dumb look on my face.

"Paint? Pastels? Pen and ink? Papier-mâché? Clay? Collage?" Mrs. Hatfield asked. "How would you like to express yourself?"

I looked around the art room. Everything looked interesting. It was almost like I had too many choices, so I couldn't pick one. I took a chair at an easel between two girls who were copying pictures they had cut out of magazines. They introduced themselves as Mia and Mackenzie.

"Does this look like Picasso to you?" Mia asked me.

"Yeah, *Joe* Picasso," Mackenzie said, cracking up at her own joke.

"You don't go here, do you?" Mia asked me. "You look too young."

"I'm in the middle school," I told her.

"Ugh, I *hated* middle school!" Mackenzie moaned. "I couldn't wait for it to end."

"Middle school was the worst three years of my life," Mia added. A few other girls, who were just arriving, agreed.

Mia and Mackenzie regaled me with horror stories from their middle-school years as Mrs. Hatfield got me paints and a brush. Their stories sounded a lot like what I was experiencing. The only difference was that they were able to laugh at them.

I was a little hesitant to ruin a perfectly good piece of white paper by putting paint on it, but Mrs. Hatfield told me that was silly.

"Express yourself," she kept saying.

The Impressionist painters, I had learned from *The History of Modern Art*, used bright colors to show how light fell on objects. Mia was wearing a yellow shirt, so I dipped my brush into the yellow paint and dabbed it on the paper. I worked to make the blotch look like a shirt. Then I began to work on Mia's pants, arms, face, and feet.

It wasn't exactly Claude Monet or anything, but you could definitely tell it was a person. Mrs. Hatfield kept coming over to compliment me and offer suggestions. Mia asked if she could have the painting when I finished it.

I was so absorbed in my painting that I almost forgot about Ellie. At three-thirty, she peeked her head in the door. "Something told me I'd find you in here," she said when she saw me.

Mrs. Hatfield told me I could continue working on my painting next time. I thanked her, said good-bye to Mia and Mackenzie, and followed Ellie outside.

"Is art your thing?" Ellie asked as we got in the car.

I had never thought of myself as having a "thing." Other kids always said music or dance or sports or computers was their thing. I never had any *thing* I was really devoted to.

"Yeah," I agreed, as I put my hair up in a pony-tail. "I think art is my thing."

"It's good to have a thing," Ellie said. "If you don't have a thing, drugs and alcohol and getting into trouble become your thing."

Ellie drove us to the abandoned YMCA. She told me that after she discovered soccer was her thing, it changed her life. She had something to care about, something she could work to get better at. It helped her make friends, and it gave her something to do. Anytime she was bored, she said, she'd just go out and dribble a soccer ball.

We climbed through the fence and into the first-floor windows of the YMCA. Ellie could see I was struggling to walk and asked what was the matter. I told her how sore I was from taking all those shots the day before.

"That's good," Ellie said. "It means you're exercising muscles you're not acccustomed to using."

We climbed down into the swimming pool and she pulled two soccer balls out of her gym bag. Then she stopped.

"Tell you what," Ellie said, putting the balls away. "Seeing as how you're so sore, I'm going to give your legs a little rest today. Let's just talk."

"About what?" I asked.

"About goalkeepers. Did you ever hear the expression 'know thine enemy'?"

"Yeah."

"There are a few basic things you need to know

about us keepers. Carmen Applegate—the keeper for the Kick—she's good. A real pro. When you run up to that ball for your shot, she's going to be in the ready position."

Ellie stood between the chalk marks she had drawn on the side of the pool. She was leaning forward slightly, her legs a little bent. She seemed relaxed, but ready to pounce.

"She'll be in the middle of the goal," Ellie continued. "Obviously, she can cover the most ground in either direction that way. She'll keep her hands away from her body."

"Why?" I asked.

"Then she won't have to move them so far when she reaches for the ball," Ellie explained. "Also, it makes her look bigger. It creates the illusion that she fills the goal."

"Is she allowed to move from side to side?"

"Yes, as long as both of her feet are on the goal line. But she can't move forward until after the ball is kicked. If she does, it's a foul. You'll get to shoot again if the referee catches her doing that."

"Why would she want to step forward?"

"It narrows the angle you have to shoot at," Ellie

told me. "It gives her a better chance of blocking the shot."

"What happens if Carmen touches the ball but it still goes in?"

"You win a million bucks," Ellie grinned. "If your shot bounces off Carmen and into the net, you win. If your shot bounces off the crossbar or goalpost and into the net, you win. If the entire ball crosses the goal line for *any* reason, you win. But as I said, Carmen is a good keeper. Chances are that if she gets a hand on the ball, she'll deflect it away from the goal."

"Is that why most goalies are tall?" I asked.

"That's right," Ellie agreed. "We can cover more ground if we're tall to begin with. But being tall isn't enough. A keeper has to be quick, and have great instincts. When I'm in a game, shots are coming at me from different speeds and different angles. I have to make instant decisions. I have to be able to dive, jump, or stretch in any direction. Believe me, shooters are not going to kick the ball right at me. They're aiming for the corners."

Ellie glanced around and lowered her voice. I looked around too, thinking maybe somebody else was there. But the big old YMCA building was completely empty except for me and Ellie.

"I'm going to tell you some things that I don't even tell my own teammates," Ellie said, almost in a whisper. "Because one day I might have to face one of them in a game."

I leaned a little closer to hear what she had to say.

"Some people think you have to be crazy to be a keeper," Ellie said. "The truth is, a good keeper is a master psychologist. She's a mind reader."

"What do you mean?"

"When you get out on that field, Carmen Applegate is going to be watching you very closely every second. She'll be looking at your eyes to see if you're peeking at your target. So don't peek! She'll be looking at the angle you approach the ball. If you come at a sharp angle, she'll know you're probably aiming for the left corner. If you approach the ball straight up the middle, she'll know you're probably aiming for the right corner. She'll be looking at how you lean your body. And when you kick the ball, she'll be looking at the position of your foot. You've got to bring your foot back to shoot, and she will be watching it very closely. She might sway back and forth just to confuse you. She might stick out her tongue at you or shout something just before you kick the ball. She might take a little too much time getting ready, just to throw off your rhythm. Keepers do that. It's a psych job."

"I think she tried to psych me out at the press conference," I said, "and again when I bumped into her at the bookstore the other night."

"You can psych her out, too," Ellie noted. "When you stand there getting ready to take your kick, look at her. See if she's leaning just a little to one side. Maybe she thinks you're going to kick it to that side. Or maybe she only *wants* you to think she thinks you're going to kick it to that side. You can glance at one corner of the goal as if you're going to shoot there, and then smack it into the other corner to fake her out. You have the element of surprise working for you. It's your best weapon. Carmen has never seen you play before. She doesn't know anything about you and she has no idea what you will do. Remember this—a shot isn't just a shot. It's a mind game. It's psychological warfare."

My head was spinning. The few times I had flipped through the channels on TV and seen a few minutes of soccer, it looked like one big bore. It was always just a bunch of players running down the field one way, and then the other team would run the ball down the field the other way. I had no idea the game was so complicated. And the only thing Ellie had talked about was a simple twenty-yard shot! The other parts of the game, she told me, would take years to understand.

Ellie pulled into my driveway and waved to my mom, who was waiting on the porch.

"I'd really like to pay you," I said as I got out of the car. "I'm sure there are better things you could be doing with your time than coaching me."

"Forget it," Ellie replied. "It's fun."

"Well, I want you to know that it really means a lot to me that you're helping me."

"You're getting more confident," Ellie told me. "I can see it in your eyes. You can make this shot."

"Do you really think so?"

"Sure. If you believe it, you can achieve it. That's what Coach Bradley tells us. You should say that to yourself all the time."

"If you believe it, you can achieve it."

"Good. Now go take your hundred shots."

"Do I have to?" I moaned, remembering suddenly how sore my legs felt.

"Only if you want to score," Ellie said as she pulled out of the driveway.

CHAPTER 15

Who in the World Is Carmen Applegate?

A week later, Briana came rushing into the kitchen waving a newspaper. It was the sports section of *The Daily Oklahoman*, which nobody else in the family reads. She showed me and Mom this short article:

OK GOALIE TO GET THE BOOT?

By BOBBIE FRISK

OKLAHOMA CITY, May 2: Is Carmen Applegate, longtime goalkeeper of the Oklahoma City Kick, on her way out?

Applegate has given up more goals this season than ever before, and, at 34 years old, is well past her prime as a professional athlete. Rumors are swirling around that the Kick are on the lookout for a younger woman to keep the ball out of their net.

"Carmen is a key player on this team," insists Kick General Manager Ed Capozzoli. "We have no immediate plans to replace her."

The usually talkative Applegate was not available for comment.

"So she was telling you the truth!" Briana exclaimed. "She wasn't trying to psych you out after all! They really *are* trying to get rid of her."

"I feel terrible!" I said. "I thought I had figured her out."

"Just because they print a rumor in the paper, that doesn't make it true," my mother said. "Maybe that general manager guy is telling the truth."

"It's obvious that he's lying," Briana insisted. "Anytime they say they have no plans to replace somebody, you can bet they already have a replacement lined up."

My father came in at that point. We showed him the article and he read it carefully.

"I'll tell you what I think," he finally said. "I bet Carmen Applegate *planted* that story in the paper herself."

"What?!"

"Sure," he continued, "it's just another one of

her psych-outs. She figured somebody would show you the article and you'd feel sorry for her. Oh, she's a smart one!"

We all looked at Dad. He might be completely off the mark. But then again, what if he was right?

"I don't know what to think anymore," I said.

CHAPTER 16

Practice Makes Perfect

I remember the exact moment I realized I really could kick a soccer ball.

It was about three weeks after Ellie had started coaching me. I had calculated that I'd taken more than 2,000 shots at the garage door by then, half to the left side and half to the right. The door is made of twelve wooden panels, with three rows going up and four panels across.

Instead of simply aiming for the left side or the right side, I decided to aim my next shot for the top panel on the left side. I took five steps back from the ball, ran up to it, and fired. The ball hit directly on the spot I intended it to hit.

A powerful sense of satisfaction swept over me. I had decided I was going to do something, and I had *done* it. It felt good to be good at something. I pumped my fist and hoped nobody walking by my house noticed.

In the beginning, I hadn't even been able to get the ball off the ground. But the more I practiced, the better I was able to direct the ball to the left, right, up, or straight along on the ground.

Each day, I felt myself getting a little bit better. I could see it in the miles per hour I was registering on Ellie's machine—thirty . . . forty . . . fifty miles per hour—and I could see it in the smudge marks on the garage door where the ball had hit repeatedly. My sister Briana painted a bull's-eye on each side of the door. I enjoyed challenging myself to see how many times I could hit them in ten shots.

The better I got at kicking the ball, the more fun it was. In the beginning, taking those hundred shots at the garage door every day was a chore. I had to force myself to do it. But once I started having some success, I began to look forward to these practice sessions.

My legs were getting stronger. It no longer hurt when I got out of bed in the morning. My concentration was getting sharper. I didn't know if I would be able to get a shot past Carmen

Applegate, but at least I no longer felt like I was going to make a total fool of myself.

At the same time, my painting was improving. Even on days when Ellie wasn't available to practice with me, I went to the Art Club at the high school. I brought some of my artwork home and Mom had it framed.

In my school, the NASCAR idiots were still giving me a hard time, but I just didn't care about them as much. No matter what they said or did to me, I knew that in a few hours I could go home, create something interesting at the Art Club, and take my shots at the garage. I was actually starting to look forward to it.

It was the end of May, and the school year was winding down. There was only a week left before I would be taking the Million Dollar Kick. Ellie said she had seen construction equipment over by the YMCA building, so we had practice in my driveway.

"Show me your stuff," Ellie said after we had done some stretching exercises.

I wanted to impress her, so I aimed for the upper left-hand panel of the garage door. The ball just missed, nicking the edge of the garage and ricocheting into the yard.

"Nice!" Ellie shouted, clapping her hands. "You know, a lot of shooters think it's cool to knock the ball into the upper corners of the goal. That's fine if you do it. But it gives you very little margin for error."

"What do you mean?"

"Nobody's perfect," she said, opening her gym bag. "Nobody can hit a target every time. Remember, you're only going to get *one* shot. If you aim for the corner and you make a tiny mistake, you get nothing. You want to get the ball into the net. That's what counts. An eighty-mile-per-hour shot is impressive. But if you try a little too hard and the ball sails over everything, that velocity didn't do you any good. A ball that trickles past the goal line counts just as much as a ball that rockets in."

"But you told me to aim for the sides," I said. "Fifty shots to the right and fifty to the left."

"That's to sharpen your accuracy," Ellie explained as she pulled a bunch of empty soda cans out of her gym bag. "Let's play some Sock Bowl."

Briana had come out of the house, munching a

peanut-butter-and-jelly sandwich. "Whatcha doing?" she asked.

"Sock Bowl is a combination of bowling and soccer," Ellie explained. Kneeling in front of the garage door, she placed ten soda cans in a triangle the way bowling pins are set up. "Okay, Whisper, see how many you can knock down with one kick."

I placed the ball on the X mark and took five steps back. The ball had to be hit low to the ground and right up the middle. I aimed and fired. It was a good shot, just a little to the right. The ball only hit the can on the far right, and it went clattering off into the bushes.

"Not so easy, is it?" Ellie laughed.

"Can I try?" Briana asked.

I wasn't crazy about the idea of Briana horning in on my practice time, but it was only a game so I decided to let her take a shot or two. Ellie retrieved the can I'd knocked over and put it back in its place.

"Watch this!" Briana said, as she got set to take a shot. I thought the ball was going to miss everything, but it nicked the can on the far left and knocked it over.

"My turn!" Ellie shouted.

"No fair!" Briana said, running over to pick up the fallen can. "Ellie plays on the high school team."

"She's a goalie, though," I said.

"Yeah," Briana cracked. "She probably can't shoot to save her life."

Ellie just laughed as she stepped back for her shot. She whacked the ball right up the middle, hitting the front can solidly. Soda cans went flying all over the place. Briana and I dove out of the way, giggling hysterically.

I tried to remember the last time Briana and I had laughed and played together. I thought it had been when I was eight and she was five.

While we were setting up the cans for the next shot, a minivan pulled up to the front of the house and some people got out. Lately, neighbors and people walking by had been stopping to watch me practice. In the beginning it was a little uncomfortable having an audience, but as I got better it didn't bother me so much. Every so often somebody would shout, "Go get 'em, Whisper!" or something like that.

But the people getting out of the minivan were not neighbors. They were hauling cameras and microphones. I recognized the lady reporter who had interviewed me the day after I won the contest.

"Hi, Whisper!" she said cheerily as she marched up the driveway. "Do you remember me? Bobbie Frisk with *The Daily Oklahoman*. I also work for NewsChannel Four. I was wondering if I could do a follow-up story on you for the paper and the TV news."

I really didn't want to be interviewed again. The last time I had spoken with her I'd said some dumb things and she had printed them. The kids at school had made fun of me and all the girls on the soccer team except for Ellie hated me. But the camera guys had already lugged a lot of equipment out of the minivan, and I thought I would look like a jerk if I said no.

"I guess so," I said reluctantly. I looked to Ellie for advice, but she had stepped out of the way with Briana and put a hand over Briana's mouth to prevent her from hogging the camera.

"I'm standing next to Whisper Nelson," Bobbie Frisk said as a guy stuck a camera in my face and dangled a huge microphone on a pole over my head. "One week from today Whisper will be taking the Million Dollar Kick at Taft Stadium. This is an unusual training method you use, Whisper. Do you mind telling us about it?"

"It's called Sock Bowl," I said, glancing at Ellie. "It's a combination of soccer and bowling. You try to knock down as many cans as possible. It sharpens your accuracy."

"I bet it does!" Bobbie Frisk said, with phony announcer enthusiasm. "Will you show us how you do it?"

I put the ball down on the X mark. I'm really going to look like a jerk if I miss everything, I thought as I stepped back five paces. The kids at school are going to torture me.

"Go for it, Whisper!" somebody called from the street, where a small crowd had gathered to watch. They started clapping rhythmically.

It was too late to turn back. I focused on the can in the front, took a run up to the ball, and fired. I looked up just in time to see that the ball was on target. It hit the front can on the right side, which sent it sailing left to knock down four or five cans. The ball continued straight and mowed down the rest. I jumped up in the air with excitement.

"Wow!" Bobbie Frisk exclaimed when the cheering had died down. "I thought you told me you never played soccer before."

"I've been practicing," I replied.

"It shows!" she bubbled. "Now Whisper, we both know Carmen Applegate, the goalie for the Oklahoma Kick, is going to be facing you in the goal next Sunday. It all comes down to aiming for her left side or her right side, am I correct? Where are you going to kick the ball?"

"I don't know," I replied.

"Come on, Whisper, how about a clue?"

"Honestly, I don't know."

It was the truth. I hadn't decided where I would kick the ball. And even if I *had* decided, I wasn't about to say it on TV. I'm no fool. Ellie had told me that the element of surprise was my strongest weapon. If Carmen Applegate knew where I was going to kick the ball, I wouldn't stand a chance.

"Well, whichever side you decide to go for, we wish you the best of luck, Whisper. This is Bobbie Frisk, of NewsChannel 4. We'll be watching, so *you* be watching."

CHAPTER 17

Instant Replay

"Whisper's gonna be on TV!" Briana shrieked. "Whisper's gonna be on TV!"

She ran around the house like a maniac, hustling Mom and me into the living room to watch. Dad, who was trying to sleep off a round-trip flight to Hong Kong, even ambled into the living room.

"You're famous!" Briana screamed when my face came on the screen.

We all watched with fascination as the camera zoomed in on the soda cans just before I kicked the ball and sent them flying in all directions. I was embarrassed, but pleased at the same time. Over the years my family had spent *hours* watching dull videos of Briana's soccer games, Briana's basketball games, Briana's dance recitals, and Briana's school plays. Now, for a change, we were watching *me*.

About a millisecond after the news segment was over, the telephone rang.

"I just saw you on TV!" the voice said excitedly. "You were great!"

It took a moment to recognize Jess's voice. I had been pretty busy practicing my kicks the last couple of weeks and hadn't thought about him very much. When I did think about him, I wondered if he liked me—or had he created that soccer simulation on his computer just for the fun of it?

"Did you tape it?" I asked Jess. "My grandmother would love to see it."

"No, but it gave me an idea," Jess replied. "I've got a video camera. I could film you kicking the ball, then you could use the tape to see what you're doing right, see what you're doing wrong. You know, analyze your form."

"I guess so." I wasn't all that interested in analyzing my form, but I didn't want to seem ungrateful. And I did want to see Jess.

"When do you want to do it?" he asked.

"My coach is coming over to work with me in a few minutes. . . ."

"I'll be right over."

Jess and Ellie arrived almost at the same time. I

introduced them to each other, telling Ellie that Jess was my friend.

"Friend, huh?" she whispered while Jess set up his video camera on a tripod next to the garage. "I say he's more than a friend."

"Shut *up!*" I giggled.

"What's the matter?" Ellie laughed. "He's cute!"

When Jess told us he was ready to film me, Ellie picked up two soccer balls and tossed one to me. I put it down on the X mark.

"Okay," Ellie shouted. "Fifty shots to the left and fifty shots to the right. Alternate sides. Focus. Concentrate. Go!"

One by one, I took my shots. If the ball bounced back to me, I put it back on the X and kicked it again. If it bounced away, Ellie would retrieve it and flip it to me. Every few kicks she would offer a suggestion, point out a flaw, or simply say something encouraging. After twenty shots or so, I was getting into a groove.

"Man, you're good!" Jess exclaimed. He seemed genuinely impressed. "Carmen Applegate doesn't stand a chance against you."

"Are you getting all this on tape?" Ellie asked.

"Oh, yeah."

Around the thirtieth shot, Mom rolled out on the porch and offered us drinks. I told her I wanted to wait until I'd finished my hundred shots. She stayed on the porch to watch.

I started getting tired after fifty shots. By the seventieth shot, sweat was pouring off me. Ellie tossed me a rag so I could wipe my face. By number ninety-nine, I was exhausted.

"Okay, one last shot," Ellie hollered. "Pretend this is the Million Dollar Kick."

I wiped my face with the towel again and placed the ball on the X mark. Stepping back, I closed my eyes and tried to summon the energy I would need for one more solid kick. I ran up to the ball and hit it as hard as I could.

It was a good shot, to the left of center and about six feet off the ground. It felt like it must have been fifty-five or sixty miles per hour. The ball slammed into the middle of the top left panel of the garage door.

Then, to my amazement, the ball smashed *through* the garage door and both the ball and the panel clattered on the hood of the car inside.

"What a rocket!" Jess hollered. "You knocked it right through the door!"

The three of us looked up at my mother sitting on the porch.

"I'll pay for it!" I promised. "I'm sorry! It was an accident!"

But Mom didn't look angry with me. In fact, she had a look in her eye that I'd seen before. It was the look she always had when Briana had scored a goal, hit a home run, or sank a basket.

"Awesome shot!" she said, clapping her hands.

Jess, Ellie, and I went inside for cold drinks, buzzing about how I had knocked out one of the garage-door panels.

"I say you're ready for Carmen Applegate," Ellie told me. "If you're not ready now, you'll never be."

While we drank, Jess rewound the tape in his video camera and hooked the camera up to his laptop computer. It would have taken anyone in my family a year to figure out how to hook all the wires up, but to Jess it was like plugging in a hair dryer.

"This was your first shot," Jess said as the image of me running up to the ball appeared on his computer screen. He advanced the image frame by frame, so we could examine it in stop action. Jess showed us how he could speed up the movement, slow it down, and even zoom in on my foot.

"See the way your right ankle isn't locked here?" Ellie pointed out. "That's why the ball sailed off to the left."

Jess went through the tape, kick by kick. Sometimes Ellie would make a comment, but mostly she just watched.

"What's that?" Jess suddenly asked, pointing at the top of the screen.

"What's *what*?"

"See the window of the apartment building across the street behind you? It looks like there's a guy in there."

Ellie and I leaned closer to the computer screen to get a better look. The background was fuzzy.

"I don't see anybody," I said.

"Maybe it's a painting on the wall of the room," Ellie guessed. "You know, a portrait of somebody."

Jess fast-forwarded through a few more kicks, his face very close to the screen. "No, the face moved a little bit," he said. "There's definitely somebody there."

"So what?" I asked. "Lots of people have come around to watch while I was practicing."

"If he wants to watch he can come outside," Jess mused.

"Maybe he's shy," I suggested.

"Can you make the image any sharper?" Ellie asked.

Jess fooled with the mouse and clicked a few keys on his computer to zoom in on the window of the apartment building. The guy in the window had something in his hand.

"It looks like he's holding a camera," Jess said.

"Do you think he was filming me, too?"

"Could be," Jess replied.

"It's still fuzzy," Ellie pointed out.

"I just got this cool new software that can digitally enhance the image," Jess said, his fingers flying over the keyboard. He enlarged the image again, and now the apartment building window filled the computer screen.

"It's a woman!" Jess said excitedly.

"Looks familiar," I added.

"I know who it is!" Ellie exclaimed. "That's Carmen Applegate!"

CHAPTER 18

Pure Science

Knowing that Carmen Applegate, the goalie for the Oklahoma City Kick, had been spying on me, really shook me up. How long had she been watching, I wondered? What had she learned about me? What was she planning?

"There's nothing illegal about scouting your opponent," Ellie informed me. "The pros do it all the time. Even high-school teams keep an eye on the teams they're going to be playing."

"Yeah, but it's kind of creepy," I replied.

"Carmen's scared," Jess said with a grin. "That's why she was filming you. She's afraid of you. Afraid you're going to score on her. Take it as a compliment."

My family agreed. Dad said that if a professional goalie like Carmen Applegate would go through the time and effort to get a room and hide in the building across the street from our house so she could secretly film me practicing, she must have been pretty worried that I was going to score on her. That should build up my confidence, he told me. If Carmen Applegate was that insecure, it meant I had a good chance to make the kick. I wasn't sure that I believed it, but it sounded good anyway.

I figured that I would practice on Friday after school and all day Saturday to get ready for the Million Dollar Kick on Sunday. But as Ellie was getting ready to leave, she broke the news to me that she had to go away for the weekend. Her grandmother who lived in Texas had taken sick, and Ellie wanted to be with her. She wouldn't get to see me take the Million Dollar Kick.

"What am I going to do?" I complained. "I need you to be there."

"Remember what I said," Ellie reminded me. "If you believe it, you can achieve it. Got that?"

"Yeah," I agreed reluctantly.

"Okay, this is your homework. Take your usual hundred shots tomorrow. But I don't want you to think about soccer at all on Saturday."

"Huh?"

"I just want you to relax, take it easy. Go to a quiet, peaceful place. Rest up. Don't answer the phone. Don't answer the door. Don't talk to any reporters. And whatever you do, don't touch a soccer ball."

There's one place I go when I want peace and quiet—the woods a few blocks from my house. I made myself a sandwich and brought along my journal and *The History of Modern Art*, which was so big it barely fit inside my backpack.

I found my favorite tree, one where the roots at the base form a smooth scoop that my back fits into perfectly. I opened my book and began to leaf through the pages.

Some of the paintings were reproduced small, in black and white, while others were full-color plates that filled the page. Every time I opened *The History of Modern Art*, it took me to another world.

Impressionists and Expressionists. Cubists and Fauves. Op art and Pop art. Manet and Monet. Picasso and Matisse. Jackson Pollock and Andy Warhol. Every time I looked at the pictures, I saw something I had never noticed before. No matter how many times I leafed through the book, I never got tired of it.

Ellie was right. Getting away from soccer and the Million Dollar Kick was the best thing I could do for myself. It was so quiet and peaceful out in the woods.

I had been sitting under the tree for several hours when I heard footsteps.

Quickly, I closed the book and stuffed it into my backpack. In all the times I had come out to these woods, I had never seen another soul. I just assumed nobody else knew about this place.

Suddenly I was frightened. It wasn't safe for a kid to be alone in the woods. I should have borrowed my mother's cell phone, it occurred to me. Too late now.

The footsteps were getting louder. They were definitely coming my way. I peeked around the tree to see if I could catch a glimpse of who was approaching. Maybe if I stayed on one side of the tree, he would pass by and never notice I was there.

It was Jess.

He was carrying his laptop computer in one hand and some other equipment around his neck.

He was looking up at the trees as he walked, as if he were bird-watching or something.

"Jess!"

"Whisper! What are you doing here?"

"I come here all the time," I told him. "What are *you* doing here? What's that, a tape recorder?"

"Yeah," he replied, a little embarrassed.

"Are you taping birdcalls?" I asked. It sounded like the kind of oddball thing he might be into.

"No . . . you'll just laugh."

"I won't," I promised. "Really."

"Okay," he said, sitting on the ground next to me. "Did you ever hear the expression, 'If a tree falls in the forest and nobody is there to hear it, does it still make a sound?'"

"Uh, yeah. I guess."

"Well, a couple of those trees over there look like they might be dead. They could fall down any minute. So I was thinking if I set this tape recorder up and went away, I might be able to capture the sound of a tree falling in the forest even if nobody is there to hear it. That is, of course, if the tree *does* make a sound when it falls. If it *doesn't* make a sound, the tape will be blank. In either case, I will have figured out whether a tree falling in a forest makes a sound in the absence of a human witness."

I burst out laughing.

"You said you wouldn't laugh!" Jess protested. He looked hurt.

"I'm sorry," I said, putting a hand on his shoulder. "It's just that you are . . . such a *genius*."

Jess looked like he wasn't sure if I meant it, or if I was just making fun of him. I reached out and stroked the curly hair that fell over his forehead.

"Nobody else would think of doing that experiment," I told him. "Nobody else would think of inventing a solar-powered flashlight. You're a scientist, an artist, and I honestly think that you're brilliant."

Then I leaned over and kissed him.

I don't know what came over me. Sometimes you just do something and think about it later. Jess flinched a little, probably out of shock. I kind of missed his lips and we bumped noses. It was probably the clumsiest kiss in the history of kissing. But after all, I was only a beginner.

"What was that for?" Jess asked, all red in the face.

"I don't know," I replied.

Jess paused for a moment, thinking things over.

"I better write up my findings," he replied.

"Me, too."

He took out his laptop, I took out my journal, and we started writing.

By the time I got home from the woods, the wind was kicking up and the skies had turned threatening. A sprinkle of rain was falling as I ran in the house. And who would be sitting on our living-room couch across from my mother but Carmen Applegate.

"What are *you* doing here?" I asked.

"I just wanted to talk about tomorrow," she replied. "May I speak with Whisper alone, Mrs. Nelson?"

Mom retreated to the kitchen and I took a seat across from Carmen.

"I have a confession to make," she began. "I did something that was very wrong."

I'll say, I thought to myself. You spied on me and played with my mind. But that's not what she said.

"I made a bet," she sighed. "I bet one of my teammates that you couldn't score on me."

"So?"

"The bet was for five thousand dollars, Whisper, and I don't have five thousand dollars."

"If you block my kick tomorrow, you'll win the money."

"Yes," she said. "But if I don't block your kick, I'll be in big trouble. And from what I hear, you've become quite a shooter in the last few months."

I had a feeling where this discussion was heading, and I didn't like it.

"Are you suggesting," I said, "that I miss my shot on purpose tomorrow so you won't lose your bet?"

"No," she said immediately. "I have a proposal for you, Whisper. And it's just the opposite of what you said. You take your best shot tomorrow. I'll make sure the ball goes in the net. I'll lose my bet. Then, when they pay you the million dollars, you give me five thousand to pay off the bet."

I thought about Carmen's proposal. It might be illegal, but I wasn't sure. Certainly, it would be an easy way for me to make a million dollars, and all it would cost me would be five thousand. I wouldn't even have to kick the ball hard. I could just lob it toward the goal and she would let it roll into the net. I wouldn't even have to worry about aiming for a corner or anything.

But what if her proposal was a lie? Maybe she was trying to get me to kick a soft shot. Then she could just ignore any secret deal we made and block my shot easily. Maybe she had never even *made* a bet with one of her teammates, it occurred to me. Maybe she was just trying to psych me out, like the other times.

"How do I know this isn't one of your tricks?" I asked Carmen. "Like when you told me you had two kids even though you don't have any kids? Like when you told me not to be distracted by the background in the stadium? Like when you secretly videotaped me practicing from the apartment across the street?"

She opened her eyes wide at that.

"Videotape? I don't know what you're talking about," she said, and I knew it was a lie.

"Look, I have a proposal for you," I said getting up from my seat. "I'll kick the ball, and you see if you can stop it. Whoever wins, wins. What do you think of *that* proposal?"

"Fine," Carmen said, gruffly. She got up from the couch and went to the front door.

"Tell me one thing," I said, opening the door

for her. It was raining heavily now. "Are the Kick really going to get rid of you if you don't block my shot, or was that just a way to psych me out?"

"We'll find out tomorrow," she said, and ran to her car through the pouring rain.

CHAPTER 19

The Big Day

Finally, June 5—the day of the Million Dollar Kick—had arrived. I set my alarm clock for nine in the morning. We had to be at Taft Stadium by eleven o'clock and I didn't want to oversleep.

It wasn't a problem. It had rained heavily during the night. A real frog-strangler, as they say around here. I had trouble sleeping with all the wind and noise on the roof. I woke up at six-thirty and couldn't go back to sleep. All I could think about was the face of Carmen Applegate staring at me, *daring* me to try to kick the ball by her.

Ellie had said I was as ready as I would ever be. Together, we had formulated a plan based on Jess's computer simulation. I was going to try to kick the ball within two feet of the right post. It didn't matter if the ball was on the ground or up in the corner. If I kicked it hard enough, it would be impossible for Carmen Applegate to block the shot.

Ellie told me to visualize myself kicking the goal. That is, I was supposed to close my eyes and imagine running up to the ball, kicking it, and watching the shot go into the net. I lay in bed a long time doing that.

As I got dressed, I felt something like the way I feel before a big test at school. My stomach wouldn't settle down. My hand trembled slightly as I squeezed toothpaste on my toothbrush.

I didn't want to look in the mirror, but I had to. The hideous multicolor soccer uniform the Kick had given me fit well enough. I turned around and looked over my shoulder to see DONUT CITY across the back with a big number one below it, followed by six little zeroes shaped like doughnuts.

I look like I'm wearing a bad Halloween costume, I thought. The people who run Donut City probably figured I'd be so humiliated to be seen in this getup that I would miss the shot and they wouldn't have to pay me a dime.

I put on the cleats Mom had given me, put my hair in a ponytail, and went down to the kitchen.

"You look like a real jock!" Briana marveled through a mouthful of Shredded Wheat.

"I *feel* like a real *jerk*."

Mom was flipping through the channels on the kitchen TV, worrying out loud that maybe the field would be too wet from the rain to play soccer. There was no word about that, but the lady on the news was talking about a tornado that had touched down somewhere in Oklahoma City. She was walking down the middle of a street, and all the houses on one side of the street had been ripped right out of the ground. On the other side of the street, the houses were untouched. It was pretty amazing to see.

". . . Twelve houses in the Windsor Hills section of northwest Oklahoma City were completely destroyed. No deaths have been reported yet, but twenty-three people were seriously injured, including Carmen Applegate, the goalkeeper of the Oklahoma City Kick soccer—"

"Did you hear that?" Briana shouted. "Carmen—"

"Shhhhhh!"

"—Applegate sustained a concussion and broken leg when a section of her roof collapsed. She is in stable condition at St. Anthony Hospital. More on this . . ."

Briana, Mom, and I looked at the screen, then at each other. I don't know what they were thinking, but I have to admit my thoughts were not entirely on Carmen Applegate's condition. They were on *my* condition.

If Carmen was in the hospital, I figured, the Million Dollar Kick would be canceled! The pressure would be off me. I could relax, have a bowl of cereal, and go back to sleep.

Mom was on the phone right away, calling the offices of the Oklahoma City Kick. She got a few busy signals before she was able to get through. The person at the other end of the line must have done all the talking, because Mom mostly said "uh-huh" and "um-hmm."

"What did they say?" Briana asked anxiously when Mom hung up the phone.

"They said, 'the show must go on.'"

I dropped my spoon into the cereal bowl.

"Who's the backup goalie for Carmen Applegate?" I asked Briana. She has been to plenty of Kick games and knew the names of the players.

"I don't know," Briana replied. "They've never

taken Carmen out of a game, as far as I know."

I grabbed the phone and quickly dialed Ellie's number. The line was busy. In a panic, I dialed Jess Kirby's number. He picked up the phone himself. He hadn't heard the news about Carmen Applegate.

"What am I going to do?" I whined. "You worked out the whole plan on your computer based on Carmen Applegate, and she's in the hospital. I need a new plan. But I don't know a thing about the new goalie."

"Relax," Jess said calmly. "Stick with the plan. Don't you see? Whoever they put in the goal won't be as good as Carmen Applegate. If she was as good as Carmen, Carmen would be *her* backup. This is *good* for you. It *increases* your chances of scoring."

"Okay, okay," I said. "We'll pick you up on the way to the stadium."

I hoped Jess was right. There was no time to worry about it, because my dad came downstairs and said it was time to go. He said he wanted to leave early just in case we hit traffic or got into an accident or something.

"There's no traffic on Sunday," I told him, trying my best to delay the inevitable.

"I just want to play it safe," he replied as Briana,

Mom, and I piled into the car. My dad drives his car the same way he pilots a plane. He's always prepared for any emergency.

We picked up Jess and got on to Route 44 with no problems. As it turned out there *was* a lot of traffic on the way to the stadium. Dad was so proud of himself, repeating over and over again how glad he was that we left early.

I didn't say anything to anybody in the car. I just looked out the window and visualized my kick, just like Ellie had told me to. All I wanted was peace and quiet.

"Remember," Briana reminded me, "keep your ankle locked."

"A sixty-mile-per-hour kick should do it," commented Jess.

"And remember to follow through," Dad advised.

"Just do the best you can, Whisper," said my mom.

"Will you all please be quiet!" I exploded. "You're making me crazy!"

They stopped talking for a while, but Briana could never keep her mouth shut for very long.

"Are you nervous?" she asked.

"Of *course* I'm nervous!" I barked. "How could I not be nervous?"

"Whisper," my mother scolded. "Your sister is just trying to help."

"Hey, you know what would be cool?" Briana said. "If you ripped off your shirt after you scored the goal."

"Are you crazy?"

"That's what they do," Briana told me. "If they score a goal, they rip off their shirt."

"I don't even like to take off my shirt in front of *Mom*. Do you think I'd take it off in front of twenty-thousand strangers?"

"You wear another shirt underneath," Briana explained. "You don't just run around in your underwear."

"I don't care!"

Dad pulled off the highway and soon the stadium came into view. There was a sign out front:

SUNDAY: KICK VS. COLORADO RAPIDS
WHISPER NELSON TAKES
THE MILLION DOLLAR KICK

"Hey, look, Whisper!" exclaimed Briana. "You're famous!"

Oh, great.

There's a special gate at Taft Stadium that players and visiting celebrities use so they don't have to go through the same entrance the fans use. Dad pulled in, and when a guard asked for identification, Dad just pointed to me in the seat behind him. The guard waved us through.

Joe Fine, the guy with *The Daily Oklahoman*, was waiting for me with a bunch of flowers. I was embarrassed, and I don't even like flowers anyway, so I handed them to my mom. Mr. Fine asked me how I was feeling, and I told him that I might have to throw up. Either he wasn't listening or he didn't care, because all he said was that I should wait until the introductions were finished before I took my kick.

"Who is Carmen Applegate's backup goalie?" I asked him.

"I have no idea," he replied, as he handed my dad some tickets. "My job was just to make sure *you* were here."

It was time to say good-bye to everybody. Mom, Dad, and Jess gave me hugs and wished me luck.

"I'm sorry I snapped at you in the car," I said when Briana wrapped her arms around me. "This whole thing was your idea, and it's not fair that you aren't getting the chance to take the kick."

"Forget it," Briana said. "You're the best shot in the family now, anyway."

Mr. Fine led me through a dark tunnel under the stadium to a door that opened onto the field. When I went through it, I could see the crowd for the first time.

The place was packed. It didn't look like there was an empty seat. Mr. Fine told me twenty-thousand fans would be watching me. People were holding up signs: KICK IT WHISPER! WHISPER KICKS BUTT! SPEAK SOFTLY AND MAKE A BIG KICK! A beach ball was bouncing around the stands. There was a blimp floating over the stadium.

A murmur spread across the crowd as I was led onto the field, and then the cheering began. With every step I took it got louder. Photographers were all over me.

There was a soccer ball waiting for me at a white X mark that had been painted onto the grass. A lady in a referee uniform escorted me to the ball. The players on both teams gathered to watch from the sidelines.

"Ladies and gentlemen," the announcer boomed, quieting down the crowd. "Welcome to Taft

Stadium. Please direct your attention to the X on the grass at the east end of the stadium. The Oklahoma City Kick, in cooperation with our good friends at Donut City and *The Daily Oklahoman*, are pleased to host the first ever Million Dollar Kick Contest!"

The crowd exploded into cheers again. People were blasting air horns.

"The young lady with the big number one on her back is Whisper Nelson, a seventh-grade student at Wilson Middle School right here in Oklahoma City. If Whisper scores a goal, she will win . . ."

"One . . . *million* . . . dollars!" It was the recorded voice of Dr. Evil in those Austin Powers movies.

There were some whistles and *ooooooohs* from the crowd.

"How about loaning me ten bucks, Whisper!" somebody hollered.

"Before Miss Nelson takes her kick," the announcer continued, "the Oklahoma City Kick ask the fans to rise for a moment of silence for the victims of the tornado that ripped through the city last night."

While the hush fell over the crowd, I rehearsed in my head what I was planning to do. No matter who they put in the goal, I was determined to slam it straight and hard to the right side of the net. I wasn't going to try to put it in the top corner. That would be too risky. My plan was to aim it low. If it sailed up a few feet, I would still score.

"Thank you," the announcer said, and the crowd sat back down in their seats. "You know, soccer fans, it will take a lot more than a tornado to stop the Oklahoma City Kick, because . . ."

"THE KICK KICK BUTT!" chanted the crowd. "THE KICK KICK BUTT!"

"That's right, fans," the announcer went on, "when we received word late last night that Carmen Applegate had been injured, we thought about canceling the Million Dollar Kick Contest. Carmen hasn't missed a game in six years, and we didn't even have a backup goalkeeper. But then we remembered Oklahoma City has another great keeper. So put your hands together and give it up for the star goalie of the All State champion Rogers High School soccer team—"

And I saw Ellie Gonzales step onto the field.

CHAPTER 20

Left or Right?

"Ellie . . . Gonnnnnzzzzzzzzzzzzzzzzzales!"

Well, I just about dropped dead right there on the field.

Ellie Gonzales, my *coach*, was going to be the goalie? I thought she was visiting her sick grandmother in Texas. If I was nervous *before*, now I was a basket case. Ellie had taught me everything I *knew*. Now I would have to use what I learned to try and beat her.

My mind was racing. I wanted to score, but if I did, I would humiliate Ellie. Maybe I should miss the shot on purpose. No, that would be crazy. I had been through so much. I had taken thousands of shots preparing for this moment. I had to give it my best shot.

The crowd cheered Ellie as she trotted out on the

field, a grim look on her face. She was wearing gloves, elbow pads, and knee pads. She had smeared some black stuff under her eyes. It made her look menacing.

"You can do it, Ellie!" somebody yelled from the stands.

I looked around frantically, searching until I found my family on the sidelines.

"Stick with the plan!" Jess mouthed.

Ellie jogged right over to me, and a bunch of photographers swarmed around us like gnats, with flashes exploding.

"I thought you were in Texas," I whispered in her ear as we shook hands.

"My grandmother got better, so we didn't go," Ellie whispered back. "A guy who works for the Kick called me this morning. I tried to reach you but your line was busy."

"I was trying to call *you*," I said.

"You okay with this?"

"Yeah, you?"

"Yeah," Ellie replied. "But Whisper, I want you to know something. I'm not going to let you score just because I coached you. You're going to have to earn it."

"Ellie," I replied, "I'm not going to let you *prevent* me from scoring just because you coached me either."

"That's the way it ought to be."

We shook hands again and Ellie jogged over to the goal. The crowd began to clap its hands and stamp its feet rhythmically. Ellie rocked from left to right on the goal line.

"I know what you're going to do," she shouted at me, cupping her hands so I would hear her over the crowd noise. Now she was smiling.

"No you don't," I hollered back.

I knew she didn't know what I was going to do, because *I* didn't know what I was going to do. Ellie was watching me carefully. I knew she was looking to see if I would glance at one side of the goal. Deliberately, I stared at the left, and then I stared at the right.

"Are you trying to psych me out?" Ellie hollered.

"Sure 'nuff," I fired back. "And you're trying to psych me out, too."

This might all come down to which one of us was the better psychologist, it occurred to me as I took my usual five steps back from the ball.

The referee blew her whistle and the crowd started stamping their feet against the bleachers. I barely heard it. Everything was a blur except for me, Ellie, and the ball. It was like I was in the middle of a dream.

I still didn't know what to do. Ellie had told me my best weapon was the element of surprise. But Ellie knew everything I knew. She knew my whole plan. There was nothing I could do that would surprise her. If I stuck with the plan, she would be able to block the shot easily. I could change the plan and aim for the left side, but she might be *expecting* me to do that and dive left. And if that's what she's thinking, maybe I should stick with the *original* plan and completely fake her out.

Unless, of course, that's exactly what she was *expecting* me to do! Why do things have to be so complicated?

"Will you kick it already?" somebody shouted.

I remembered that Ellie told me she was left-handed like me, and that she moved to her left better than to her right. Maybe I should kick the ball to her right, which was my left. The question was, did she remember that she had told me that? And if she *did* remember, would she think that *I* remembered? And if she thought I'd remember, would she think I would kick to her weakness, or try and fake her out and kick it to her strong side?

It was a simple question I had to answer: left or right?

"If you're not sure what to do," Ellie hollered through her cupped hands, "just kick it up the middle!"

I had to laugh. So did Ellie. The referee blew her whistle again, like a car behind you honking for you to get moving. I couldn't wait any longer. I had to make up my mind. Left or right? There was only one way to decide.

> *Eenie meenie miney moe.*
> *Catch a tiger by the toe.*
> *If he hollers let him go.*
> *Eenie meenie miney moe . . . LEFT!*

I took a deep breath. This was the moment I had been waiting for—and dreading—since the day I entered the stupid contest months ago.

The crowd sounded like the roar of a 747 taking off.

"If you believe it," I said to myself, "you can achieve it."

I took aim at the left side of the goal, ran up to the line, and brought back my leg.

And then I kicked the ball.

CHAPTER 21

Endings

I can still see the Million Dollar Kick in my head. Just as I have a mental videotape of the time I kicked the ball into my own team's goal, I will always be able to replay the Million Dollar Kick in my mind.

I remember the way the black spots spun backward after my foot launched the ball toward the goal. I remember Ellie diving to her left, extending her arms over her head, like Superman flying across the goal line. I've watched this mental videotape hundreds of times, forward, backward, and in slow motion.

I knew from the beginning that there were three possible outcomes for the shot. In the hours we spent preparing for this moment, Ellie and I had even discussed them. . . .

1. I could make the shot. The ball goes into the net and everybody but the goalie goes home happy.

2. I could miss the goal completely. That would be the worst possible outcome. If I kicked the ball wildly, the goalie wouldn't even get the chance to make a save.

3. The goalie could block the shot. Nothing to be ashamed of. At least that would mean that I had put the ball within the dimensions of the goal.

Well, if this had been a multiple-choice test, the correct answer would have been "None of the above." What actually happened was completely different from anything we had anticipated.

CHAPTER 22

The Million Dollar Kick

As soon as the ball left my foot, I knew I had hit it well. Sometimes you just have the feeling that you have done something right.

The ball was flying left, but not so far to the left that I had any fear that it would miss the goal. It was about three feet off the ground. Perfect shot. Maybe fifty-five miles per hour.

Ellie dove for it. I wasn't sure if she had guessed correctly which side I was going to kick the ball to, or if she had waited until I kicked before committing herself to one side or the other. I was concentrating on the ball.

She hung in the air for a moment, her arms and legs fully extended. Even though she was wearing gloves, I could see that her fingers were wide open, as if she were trying to hold a pizza plate with one hand.

The ball ticked off the fingertips of her right hand and was deflected out of the goal.

"*Ohhhhhhhh!*" moaned the crowd.

I hung my head. It had been a good shot, I knew. But not good enough.

I began to second-guess myself immediately. If I had kicked the ball a little higher or a little more to the left, Ellie never would have been able to touch it. If I had kicked it to the right side instead of the left, it would have been an easy goal.

If, if, if.

I felt sorry for myself as I started off the field. At the same time, I felt good for Ellie. She had made an *unbelievable* save. People in the stands were cheering as she picked herself up off the dirt.

". . . Best stop I ever saw," somebody said.

The referee blew her whistle and made some hand signals that I didn't understand.

"Goalkeeper stepped off the line before the ball was kicked!" boomed the announcer. "Rekick!"

I was still hanging my head when I reached the sideline and noticed all the players on the Kick were waving and shouting at me excitedly.

"You get another shot!" they were hollering. "Do it again!"

"Huh?"

"She stepped off the line too early!"

I looked over at Ellie. She was nodding her head as if to say, "Yeah, they caught me."

The fans began to clap and scream again as I made my way back to the X mark, even louder than before. It lifted my spirits. They knew I had made a good shot, and they were rewarding me for it. They knew Ellie's save was brilliant too, even if she had bent the rules a bit. The fans were paying closer attention now. They wanted to see if Ellie and I could do it again.

You got yourself another chance, I told myself. Don't blow it.

"Nice shot," Ellie shouted, slapping the dirt off her jersey.

"Nice save."

Ellie had one small advantage now that she didn't have before the first shot. She knew that I had aimed the first shot at the left side. It had been a good shot. Maybe I should do the exact same thing, and bet that Ellie would not be able to make two spectacular saves in a row.

I looked at Ellie. She was staring right back at me, a little smile on her face.

On the other hand, I thought, if she was thinking the same thing that I was, then she would have
an even *easier* time blocking the second shot if I
kicked it to the left side again. Maybe I should
cross her up and kick it to the right side.

But then, what if she thinks of *that* too?

Oh, forget it.

Eenie meenie miney moe.

Catch a tiger by the toe.

If he hollers let him go.

Eenie meenie miney moe.

My

mother

says

to

pick

this

one

and

that

is

Y . . .

O . . .

U . . .

RIGHT!

The crowd was stamping their feet against the bleachers so hard that I thought the stadium might break apart. Ellie got herself set in the goal. The referee placed the ball on the X mark and blew her whistle. It was time.

I stepped back five paces from the ball and took a deep breath, trying to gather my energy and focus my concentration for one more shot.

"If you believe it," I repeated silently, "you can achieve it."

I ran toward the ball, being careful not to tip off which side I was aiming for. At the last instant, I shifted my weight a little and brought my foot down slightly on the left side of the ball to drive it toward the right. I kicked it with everything I had.

There was nothing left for me to do. No matter what happened, my day was done.

It was a good kick, but not quite as good as the first one. The ball was a little higher off the ground, but also a few inches farther from the goalpost, so Ellie wouldn't have to dive so far for it.

Ellie, making sure that she didn't jump off the line too soon again, waited a split second longer. But she guessed right again, leaping up and sideways.

Again, she got a fingertip or two on the ball.

This time, she deflected it straight up.

As Ellie completed her dive and tumbled to the ground face first, the ball bounced off the bottom of the crossbar above her. It came straight down toward her body, where she lay across the goal line.

If Ellie had landed on her back, she might have caught the ball coming off the crossbar or batted it away. But she landed on her stomach. The ball hit her on the back.

And then it rolled into the net.

"*Gooooooooooooooaaaaaaaaaaaalllllllllllllllllll-llll!!!!!!!!!!*" the announcer screamed as the crowd erupted. "*Goooooaaaaaalllllllllllllllllllll!*"

I jumped up in the air. Fireworks went off at the four corners of the field and exploded high over the stadium. Photographers surrounded me. A message on the scoreboard flashed WHISPER NELSON HAS JUST WON A MILLION DOLLARS! "We Are the Champions" blared out of the speakers. Dr. Evil kept repeating, "One million dollars! One million dollars!" People in the stands were standing, cheering, clapping, crying.

"Whisper! Whisper! Whisper! Whisper!" they chanted.

I wanted to go over to Ellie, but Briana got to me first, jumping all over me like a monkey. She took me by the hand and led me on a victory lap around the field. People were reaching out to slap hands with me, and I touched as many as I could. I saw my mom in the front row as we passed by. She was crying so hard, it looked like I had *missed* the shot.

I was searching for Ellie, but there were so many people around that I couldn't spot her. The president of Donut City—some guy with a really bad toupee—handed me a check made out for ONE MILLION DOLLARS. Photographers snapped our picture, and I was too dazed even to notice all the flashes.

Finally, Ellie found me and threw her arms around me.

"I'm sorry the ball went in," I said.

"You made two fantastic kicks," she replied. "You deserved to score."

"I couldn't have made them without you."

"You must tell me," Ellie asked, "what was your strategy? I just *have* to know. What made you decide to aim left on the first shot and right on the second shot?"

"It's a simple strategy," I revealed. "Eenie meenie miney moe—"

"I did that, *too!*" Ellie said, and we both collapsed into a fit of giggles.

While we were laughing, the coach of the Oklahoma City Kick came over and introduced herself. She was a tall, white-haired woman.

"That was a fine effort you made, young lady," she told Ellie after congratulating me.

"Thanks."

"You know, I don't have a backup keeper for Carmen Applegate. I was going to ask one of the other players to take her place today, but I was wondering if you might consider—"

"Yes!" Ellie answered quickly.

"It doesn't pay much," the coach apologized.

"I don't care!"

Ellie gave me another hug and went off with the coach to meet the members of the Kick.

Briana was still hanging all over me. It took a while for my dad to wheel my mom onto the field. In the meantime, a lady jogged over. I recognized her as Lori Bradley, the high-school soccer coach who had told me she would not coach me several months earlier.

"I just wanted to congratulate you, Whisper," Coach Bradley said, shaking my hand. "You have a good leg on you. I know that you say soccer isn't your game or anything, but I think you've got potential. I'd love for you to try out for the team when you reach high school."

"Are you joking?" I asked.

"Not at all."

"I'll consider it," I told her. "I will seriously consider it."

Coach Bradley shook my hand again and said to look her up when I got to ninth grade. As she was walking away, I ran over and stopped her.

"Coach," I said, pulling the check out of my pocket. "I want you to have this."

She looked at the check and her eyes got big.

"You mean you want me to hold on to it for you?"

"No," I repeated. "I want you to *have* it. I want to donate it to the high school."

"Are you crazy?" Briana broke in. "You're going to give away the million bucks?" Briana dashed over to my parents, probably to tell them to put me in an insane asylum.

"You're not serious," Coach Bradley said to me, very seriously.

"I *am*. Will this money be enough to make sure they never take the grass off your field and replace it with artificial turf?"

"It wouldn't take a million dollars, Whisper," Coach Bradley said. "You would still have a lot of money left over for yourself."

"Then I'll use the rest to set up a recycling program or something."

"Are you sure you want to do this, Whisper? Maybe you should think it over and talk about it with your parents."

"I don't want to think it over," I said. "It's my money, and I want to do something for the environment with it."

"Well, if it's okay with your parents, it's okay with me. On behalf of the high school athletic department, I graciously accept your generous donation. But you hold on to the check until you decide for sure what to do with it."

Briana came rushing back with my father, who was huffing and puffing as he pushed my mom's wheelchair.

"Whisper, are you sure you want to do that?" Dad asked, "Let's not make any hasty decisions—"

"It's a wonderful gesture," my mother interrupted, "and I think it's a wonderful idea." She reached out for a hug, and I gave it to her.

I wanted to stay to watch Ellie play for the Kick, but my mom was exhausted from all the excitement. As we drove home my dad was quiet—probably fuming about the money I had given away. But Mom, Jess, and Briana were buzzing about my shots on goal. They described them over and over again in excruciating detail as Jess replayed them on his computer screen again and again.

I was in a fog. There were so many thoughts going through my head.

I can't predict the future. I don't know if I'm going to try out for the soccer team when I get to high school or not. I don't know if Mom and I are going to get along any better now, either. I don't know if my sudden interest in art is going to last. And I don't know what's going to happen with me and Jess.

But I felt a warm, nonspecific feeling of goodness around me. Up until that day, the mental video that I carried in my mind everywhere had just one highlight—eight-year-old Whisper kicking the ball into her own team's goal. Now, as I watched myself on Jess Kirby's computer screen, I had a new highlight. Even if I couldn't erase the old one, it felt good to have something better to look at.

As we drove by the old YMCA building where Ellie had taken me to practice, I looked out and saw that some of the windows had new glass in them. There were cranes and bulldozers in the parking lot and the fence was gone. In its place was a large sign:

SITE OF THE *NEW* YMCA OF GREATER OKLAHOMA CITY

CHILDREN PLAYED HAPPILY IN THIS BUILDING FOR YEARS BEFORE IT WAS NEARLY DESTROYED IN THE BOMBING ON APRIL 19, 1995. SOON THEY WILL BE PLAYING HERE ONCE AGAIN. PLEASE PARDON OUR APPEARANCE WHILE WE ARE IN THE REBUILDING PHASE.

The old Y was a little bit like me, I realized. I was a pretty normal, happy kid when I was younger.

And then, when I got to sixth and seventh grade, it was like a bomb went off and devastated me. I was empty, useless, pathetic.

"Are you okay, Whisper?" my mother asked as I stared out the window.

"Please pardon my appearance," I told her. "I am in the rebuilding phase."